THE MISEDUCATION OF MISS DELILAH

School of Charm #3

MAGGIE DALLEN

1

Miss Delilah Clemmons held her teacup to her lips for a moment longer than necessary as she took a deep, fortifying breath.

The scent of tea leaves and sugar, she'd found, was far superior to the stench of illness that had permeated her family home for as long as she could remember.

"How is father?" she asked once she'd lowered her cup.

Her stepmother's voice was cold and even. "The same."

Delilah nodded. *The same.* That was the response she always got. She couldn't quite recall at what point her father's health had fallen into decline, but it often seemed as though he had been plummeting toward death for as long as she'd known him.

His mental faculties were still there and her father, the baron, still ruled over this small family and his estate with an iron fist. Metaphorically, of course. In reality, he was confined to his bed day and night, and sent orders through his wife.

His wife who despised Delilah.

Perhaps that was unfair. Maybe *despised* was too strong of a word. What the Baroness of Linden felt for her step-daughter could hardly be said—not even by Delilah. The older woman was difficult to read, but her interactions with Delilah had always been cold. There was no heat of anger, just a general sense of disdain and disapproval.

Even as a small child, Delilah had sensed it, and she had known better than to take offense. It was well understood that Delilah had failed her father horribly by not being born a boy. She supposed she'd failed her stepmother even more so.

With the estate entailed, she and her stepmother would be in a precarious position when her father passed.

Unless Delilah married well, of course.

Which she would. After all, it was the least she could do.

Besides, her father had set aside a small fortune and the one unentailed property he owned along the coast to ensure it. Whatever was not going to his heir had been tied to her dowry to ensure that she land a gentleman of means and power.

Delilah took another small sip and stole another breath of tea-scented air as a clock ticked loudly behind her.

She'd always hated this drawing room. So stiff, so dreary. Her stepmother's cloying perfume mixed with the smells of medicine and the stale scent of a house that hadn't seen sunlight or fresh air in far too long.

Altogether it made Delilah's stomach churn with unease.

From the moment Miss Grayson had informed her she'd been summoned home for a visit, she'd felt it—the clawing sensation of panic barely suppressed. At the finishing school, where she lived amongst her friends, she could ignore it. Sometimes she even managed to convince herself it was gone altogether, this unpleasant mix of fear and anticipation. The sensation that her life was about to take a turn. That she was hovering on a precipice just waiting for a good shove.

Her stepmother set down her teacup with a rattle that

seemed to shake the room. "Your father has found you a husband."

And there it was.

The air left Delilah's lungs so suddenly she felt lightheaded. A deep breath of that heavy, noxious air only made her head spin more. "Oh yes?" she said, taking another sip of tea.

It was through sheer habit that she managed to sound so cool and unemotional.

It had always been this way between Delilah and the baroness. A battle to see who could be the most contained. Which of the two beauties in this house had the most decorum.

Delilah would hardly give her stepmother the pleasure of stumbling now. She'd been training all her life for this.

The free-falling sensation that had her stomach plummeting was disguised beneath a haughty sniff and pursed lips. "And who might I be marrying?"

There. Not even Miss Grayson at the School of Charm could find fault with that delivery. She was practically the epitome of grace and nobility. She was—

"John Faring, the Baron of Everley."

For the first time since she was six, Delilah forgot to don her façade. Horror shot through her, making her blood curdle and her stomach heave. "Lord Everley."

She whispered his name, but it was the nickname her friends at school had given the man that clanged in her head like a bell. *Lord Evil.*

Silly nickname—no doubt Louisa had thought of it. The girl lived for melodrama. And yet...

Much as she tried to tell herself it was ridiculous, the nickname echoed in her skull.

Evil.

A man they called *Evil.*

This was who she was to marry.

Her stepmother's lips quirked up a bit at the corners. "I see you are familiar with the man."

Delilah stared at the baroness with lips frozen in shock. Familiar with him? The man had threatened to financially ruin Louisa's family. He'd suggested Addie's cousin should kill her little brother.

In jest, one might hope, but even so...

Her stepmother's eyes glinted with malice. Or maybe amusement.

Or perhaps with her stepmother they were one and the same. It was difficult to say. The baroness had a sort of cruel beauty about her. Half the age of the baron, she'd come from a good family and embodied excellent breeding. Fair hair and unmarked skin. Blue eyes and a spine of steel. She'd taught Delilah well in the art of gentility and manners.

Delilah called on those lessons now as she steeled herself, forcing her shoulders to lower, her lips to snap shut, and her brow to clear. "Indeed," she said, her voice pleasantly even. "I have made his acquaintance."

"Excellent," the baroness said. "He will host an engagement ball in a fortnight and the banns will be read."

"But—" The protest died on her lips as she met her stepmother's cold, malicious gaze.

But he is a monster. But they call him Lord Evil. But...what if I don't wish to marry him?

Nothing she said would change matters. If anything, it would only add to her stepmother's pleasure.

She set her cup down gently. It was not as though this was a surprise. She'd always known this day would come. This was her price to pay. After eighteen years of receiving everything a girl could wish—everything of material value, at least—it was now time to see through her duty.

"You shall be pleased to hear that Lord Everley is exceedingly wealthy," her stepmother said, all brisk business as though Delilah's life was not crashing down around her ears.

Indeed, Delilah had no doubt her stepmother was relishing this moment.

Delilah's mother had died during childbirth. Young and fragile, by all accounts, her mother had suffered numerous miscarriages and Delilah did not doubt that she suffered mightily from her father's displeasure at being left heirless.

Delilah often suspected that her mother was blessed to have died when she did, not knowing that her last act on this earth had been the greatest disappointment of all.

She'd at last delivered a child, and it had been a useless girl.

Her stepmother had been glad of it, no doubt. It gave her the chance to provide the son her father so desperately desired.

But fate was not so kind to this family.

And so it was that Delilah was given everything she wished. She was spoiled, she would be the first to admit it. Her father and stepmother handed her over to a steady stream of nursemaids, governesses, and tutors, until she'd grown old enough to attend finishing school.

All of that learning, the skills and the manners, the jewels, the balls, and the best gowns money could buy—it had all been for this.

So that she might snare a husband of great fortune.

"A baron," she mused, as though she were referring to someone else's future husband and not her own. "I thought Father had his sights set higher."

The slight twitch of the baroness's lips might have been a smile, if she were capable of such a thing. "Are you disappointed?" She eyed Delilah as though just seeing her now for the first time. "Did you expect to marry an earl?" She laughed without humor. "My, someone thinks well of herself."

She ignored the jab. Sharp words that used to prick her sensitive skin as a child, now bounced off of her skin, thanks to a thick layer of scars. "I merely meant that Father had always said—"

"Your father wished for a marriage that would ensure his family had nothing to fear financially. Lord Everley can and will provide that comfort."

She nodded. "Of course."

"Are you disappointed?" Her stepmother's voice was mild. Distantly curious, at best, as she eyed Delilah over the edge of her teacup.

Was she *disappointed*? That her father had just sold her to the highest bidder? No. That was to be expected. Was she horrified at the idea of spending the rest of her days with a man who might be more cruel than her own family?

Yes.

She met her stepmother's gaze evenly. "Of course not."

That horror, the sinking sensation, the heartache that made her chest feel too small...

She held her stepmother's gaze as she forced that all aside. She pushed it down—far, far down. So deep inside her that she was finally able to tilt her lips up in the small, satisfied smile she'd so expertly perfected when she was nine years old. "I am certain this marriage will be quite satisfactory."

A little while later, when the carriage was to be drawn 'round to return her to the school, she found she could not do it. She could not go back to the school and her friends and their kind concern.

Here in this house, facing her stepmother, she could actually believe her own words. The marriage would be satisfactory. After all, Everley was a man of means. Her father had chosen him. He might not be kind, but he was nothing she could not handle.

Delilah pushed her shoulders back and tilted her chin up.

This was what she was meant for. This was her purpose, and she would make it work.

She would build the perfect life, even if her husband wasn't the man of her choosing.

"You must be eager to return," her stepmother said. "You will wish to share your good news with your friends, I am certain."

Whether her stepmother was in earnest or taunting her was difficult to determine. Either way, it did not matter because she found she was quite incapable of moving toward the door.

After an hour of wishing to flee, she could not do it.

The thought of their reactions... The way Addie would look at her with alarm, how Prudence would scowl and pester, how Miss Grayson's eyes would fill with sympathy, how Louisa would... Well, Louisa would be Louisa.

No. She could not face their questions nor their censure.

Most of all, she could not face their pity.

"Do you know..." she started slowly. "With all the preparations that will need to be made before the wedding. Might it not be best if I stay here at home until the wedding?"

If her stepmother was surprised, she did not let on. "If that is what you wish."

It was *not* what her stepmother wished, that much was clear.

Delilah didn't much relish the idea of being under this roof again, either. But the alternative was so much worse so she said, "That is what I wish."

Her stepmother sniffed. "Then so be it."

2

Rupert Calloway might have been the second son of the Marquess of Markland, but few would ever know it.

"A Mr. Calloway is here to see you, sir."

Rupert overheard the butler as he rudely followed in the servant's wake. But really, the Earl of Tolston had been the one to summon him and had demanded he arrive in haste.

Surely he was not meant to wait in the foyer. And aside from all that...

"Rupert!" Tolston shouted his name as he bounded toward the door.

Rupert grinned. Aside from that—they were old friends.

Tolston embraced him in a hug that ended with him pounding his back. "Good to see you again." Tolston gestured for him to take a seat. "And thank you for coming at such short notice."

Rupert followed the other man into the center of the room as the butler made his exit. "For you? Anything." He fell into the seat, weary after a long day of travel. "I must admit, I was surprised at the suddenness of it all."

Tolston sank into the seat across from him with a sigh. "You know that I've been looking into Lord Everley..."

Rupert nodded, his smile fading fast as his eyes narrowed. He had a history with Everley, and Tolston knew it. "You should have brought me in from the start."

After all, this was what he did. Investigating the wrongdoings of the high and mighty had become his specialty.

Tolston gave a rueful scoff. "And put Everley on high alert? That was the last thing I wanted."

Rupert wished he could argue. These days he went about his business with subtlety and tact. Sometimes even with subterfuge. But years ago, when Everley had callously stolen his friend from him...

Well, he hadn't the wherewithal to lie low. He'd shouted his suspicions from the rooftops, making an enemy out of Everley, and destroying any chance he might have had to get close enough to destroy the man in kind.

Rupert leaned forward, resting his elbows on his knees. "Why now?" he asked. "What has changed?"

Tolston's expression hardened and he looked every bit his age and his station—no hint of the boy he'd been when Rupert first met him during their school days. "He's getting married."

Rupert's brows arched in surprise. From the way he'd said it, marriage sounded like a deadly affair. Understanding dawned. "Is his bride-to-be a friend of yours? Family, perhaps?"

Tolston shook his head. "Not quite. I've met the girl on multiple occasions, but she is a friend to my fiancée." His brows drew down into a fierce glare. "Which makes her a friend to me."

"I see," Rupert said.

Quite honestly, he did not see. He'd never been engaged,

and he wasn't certain he wished to be if it led a man to be quite so earnest about *anything.*

Rupert leaned back in his seat. "So you wish to disrupt this wedding," he surmised. "Have you thought about telling the girl's family of your suspicions about Everley?"

Tolston winced. "No. Mainly because at this point, that is all they are. Suspicions. Despite my men and I looking for evidence, everything we've found that points to Everley's cruelty is circumstantial, at best. He covers his tracks well." Tolston's lips curved up in a sneer. "Unfortunately the man's soulless use of his wealth and power, lending money to those who are too weak and vulnerable to see the sort of trap he's leading them into... It isn't enough. Cruelty is no crime, and from what I know of Delilah's father..."

"Delilah?" Rupert said.

"Miss Delilah Clemmons," Tolston said. "Only child to the Baron of Linden."

Rupert grimaced.

"I see you are familiar with him."

"Only as a passing acquaintance," Rupert said. But that was enough to know that the man was as greedy as they came. The only man who came close to Everley in terms of merciless ambition. "I'd thought the old man passed away years ago."

Tolston gave a little grunt of acknowledgement. "It seems he's been threatening to die for years now, but the old bugger won't let go." He narrowed his eyes in thought. "He won't shuffle off this mortal coil until he's certain that his family is well taken care of."

Rufus furrowed his brow in concentration as he tried to reconcile the hard old man he remembered from his youth with this image of fatherly devotion. "He's that committed to his family and their happiness, eh?"

Tolston snorted in amusement. "Good heavens, no. It's his pride at work, I'd imagine."

Rupert nodded. That was far easier to imagine. "And so he has handed over his only daughter to the devil himself to ensure that she is well taken care of."

"That is my best guess," Tolston said.

They sat in silence for a moment. Rupert couldn't speak to Tolston's thoughts, but for his part he was stewing in pity for this girl. "Young, is she?"

Tolston nodded. "Slightly younger than Addie, my bride-to-be, and Addie is nineteen."

Rupert took a deep breath and let it out slowly. He had no sisters, but he had female cousins he was close to, and he couldn't imagine allowing any of them near a gentleman like Everley. "Terrible," he muttered. "I can see why you feel a sense of urgency to stop Everley before he weds." He shook his head. "It's horrible to think of a sweet, innocent young lass in the clutches of one such as he."

Tolston's burst of laughter had Rupert's head snapping up, his eyes widening in surprise. "Did I say something amusing?"

Tolston clearly worked to sober himself as he gave his head a shake. "No, no. Of course not. It is just…" He let out another choked laugh. "It is just hard to imagine anyone describing Delilah as 'sweet' or 'innocent'."

Rupert's brows hitched up further in surprise.

"Not to say that she *isn't*…an innocent, that is," Tolston said quickly. "She is a proper young lady, of that there is no doubt."

Rupert laughed as well as he realized what his old friend was trying to say in his roundabout way. "But she is not sweet."

Tolston snickered. "Not as such, no."

Rupert arched a brow. "A bit of a cold fish?"

"I wouldn't say *that*…"

"A nag, then," he guessed. Honestly, now he was just having fun putting his old, slightly stodgy friend on the spot.

"Oh quit it," Tolston said with a huff. "I shall not speak ill of my wife's schoolmate. Despite Delilah's...haughty demeanor she has proven to be a loyal friend to Addie."

"Haughty demeanor." Rupert leapt on the phrase. That gave him a clear impression, indeed. Knowing what he knew of her father, Rupert could easily believe that the girl would be spoiled and arrogant.

And if she bore his resemblance in any way, she'd be remarkably plain, to boot. Which made him wonder... "Just what is Everley getting out of this match?"

The last of Tolston's humor faded fast. "That is exactly what I wish to know."

Rupert studied his friend. His normally stoic features were creased in concern, his posture tensed as though ready to spring into action.

Tolston was normally so calm, so unreadable and seeing him agitated was alarming. Tolston's fears were understandable if he knew the girl in question. But still...

Rupert knew from experience how dangerous it could be to be emotionally involved during an investigation. Emotions only clouded the issue, it made it impossible to act with reason and logic.

Which was why it was for the best that he'd arrived when he had. He'd learned how to keep an emotional distance while working an investigation like this one, even if there was a damsel in distress.

Especially if there was a damsel in distress.

"Has anyone tried talking to the girl herself," he said.

"Delilah? No." Tolston's brows drew down. "Addie and her friends have been trying ever since they received their invitations to the engagement ball."

"She hasn't received them?"

Tolston gave his head a quick shake. "Either she's avoiding them, or..."

Rupert made a growling sound in the back of his throat. "Or she's being kept away."

"Precisely. We don't know which, but either way, it's been impossible to get to her. To warn her or help her or..." Tolston rand a hand through his hair in impatience. "Addie is beside herself with worry, and I..." Tolston flashed a rueful, nearly desperate smile. "I'm afraid that I cannot abide that. I cannot bear to see Addie upset."

Rupert was momentarily stunned into silence. He'd never known his old friend to care about anyone or anything to this degree. But then again, he'd never seen his friend in love before, either.

Poor sap.

"When is the engagement ball?" Rupert asked.

"Two days from now."

Rupert frowned. That didn't give him much time to wrap his head around the current investigation. "And the wedding?"

"Three weeks hence."

Rupert cursed under his breath. "Then we must act quickly."

"Exactly. That is why I asked you to come. If there's anyone who knows the extent of the danger, it is you. And you know how Everley thinks, how he acts."

Rupert grunted his agreement. For better or for worse. He'd spent months trying to prove that Everley had murdered his younger cousin, Lyle. The heir to the title that Everley now bore, Lyle was Everley's rival...and Rupert's closest friend.

As good as a brother, really.

"Do you think you could help?" Tolston asked.

Rupert met his friend's gaze evenly. His heart began to pound with determination. "I will do everything in my power to bring Everley to his knees before he has a chance to wed your fiancée's friend."

Tolston's shoulders sagged with relief. "I'll do anything I can to assist you. Just tell me what you'll need."

Rupert rested back in his seat as he crossed his arms and stared into the distance, his mind racing to come up with a plan. "First and foremost..." He turned to his friend. "I'll need admittance to the engagement ball."

Tolston nodded. "Consider it done."

3

The room seemed to be spinning as Delilah made her way through the crowd.

"You look so beautiful, darling." An older woman who smelled of licorice and talcum powder kissed the air beside both her cheeks.

"Thank you," she murmured. Her hair felt too heavy, her face strained from smiling. The party had only just begun, and she already felt exhaustion creeping in.

The gown was cinched too tight, and her breath came in short bursts as she made her way slowly through the crush.

Where was she heading?

To her betrothed, she presumed. She had yet to speak to him alone. It had been weeks since she'd discovered she was engaged to Lord Evil—no, Lord *Everley*.

Blasted Louisa with her silly nicknames.

It had been weeks and she'd yet to see her fiancé.

Was that normal?

Ought not an engagement begin with a courtship?

Apparently not, as far as her betrothed was concerned.

He'd come to the house to discuss the details of her dowry, but left before she was able to see him.

Pressing business, her father's solicitor had explained when he'd come into the drawing room to make Everley's excuses.

Had he known that she'd been waiting for him?

Had he cared?

She shoved the questions aside. Likely not, and that did not matter. This was no love match, and she'd never expected it to be. Other girls might have spent their childhoods dreaming of fairy tales and romance, but not she.

She certainly would not begin now.

The room seemed to swim around her and a trickle of sweat made its way down her neck.

It was stiflingly hot in here; she couldn't breathe properly.

And the *people*.

She'd never minded crowds before, but today...tonight...

She itched to tug off her clinging gloves. She had an overwhelming urge to take off her slippers, let her hair down, and...run.

Just run.

She clasped her hands together and focused on her breathing. It was just emotions talking. Nerves, most likely. After all, it wasn't every day one attended one's own engagement party.

She looked around her, a small smile plastered in place as it had been for the past two hours. Some faces she recognized, but not many.

Everley was popular, it seemed.

Her mind flashed back to earlier in the summer when Louisa had overheard him talking.

Perhaps he wasn't popular. Maybe he was just feared. Maybe everyone here owed him something. Perhaps, like Louisa's father, these partygoers were at his mercy now that they'd handed him their fate.

Just like her father had handed him hers.

Her future rested in *his* hands now.

She sucked in a deep breath of warm, scented air as she tried to steady herself. Her chin tilted up higher, her shoulders straightened.

A secret she'd learned a long time ago...the lower you feel, the higher you hold yourself. It worked like a charm. Pride and confidence did more to earn respect—and yes, sometimes fear—than all the smiles and simpering in the world.

So now she called upon that lesson as she headed toward the French doors leading outside.

Peering gazes followed her as she walked. Of course they were interested. She was the belle of the ball...for today, at least. This was her party and she ought to enjoy it. After all, she'd never had a proper coming out. She'd never had the sort of season other debutantes enjoyed, with charming men and endless dancing...

She'd be going from the schoolroom to her marriage bed so quickly her head was still spinning.

She stood still and shut her eyes. Marriage bed. She should not have gone there, not even in her mind.

One thing at a time. That was how she would adjust to her new life.

For now, she merely had to find air. Space. A brief respite from the crush of the crowd.

She'd also prefer to do so without running into her friends from Miss Grayson's. She was still annoyed that her stepmother and Everley had planned the guest list without her.

But then again, she had little to do with this engagement or the wedding, so why start participating now?

Her stepmother was here somewhere, but Delilah was doing her best to avoid her as well. It was surprisingly easy to avoid running into Prudence, Addie, and Louisa when there were so many people trying to get close to her.

She'd pretended not to notice as they took turns frantically waving her down.

She knew what they wanted. They wanted to *save* her.

Silly girls.

As if she needed saving.

She sniffed at the thought. *Hardly*.

And besides, Everley certainly wasn't all *that* bad. He might have had his faults but it wasn't as though he'd been abusing her these past weeks. Just ignoring her. But that was hardly a crime, now was it?

Besides, every time she'd spotted him this evening, he'd worn a congenial smile. He hadn't spoken to her, but he'd smiled. She reached the edge of a crowd with a sigh. A smile had to count for something.

The doors were within reach when she spotted familiar red hair.

Drat.

Louisa was heading toward the doors as well, her betrothed hovering beside her as she laughed at something he'd said.

If Louisa managed to get her alone outside, there would be no shaking her. The girl was tenacious—and melodramatic, to boot. Delilah's insides fluttered wildly in panic at the sight of her.

So silly. No one ought to fear *Louisa*, for heaven's sake. The girl was wild, unpredictable, dramatic, and loud, but she wasn't—

Delilah turned toward the nearest hallway as her mind worked to finish that sentence.

Never mind. Perhaps one *ought* to fear Louisa for every reason she'd just listed.

After all, if there was one person to be counted on to cause a scene—intentionally or not—it was Louisa.

And all Delilah wanted right now was to get through this

engagement and her wedding with her pride intact and her head held high.

The hallway she found herself in was dark. Private quarters, no doubt. She paused for a moment, eyeing the shadows before her. She ought to turn back. She ought to rejoin the party.

And yet...

The shadows seemed to call to her. A quiet, dark, safe mirage. Surely it couldn't hurt to escape...just for a moment.

She took a step forward, fear making her pause as a voice spoke behind her. But it was a stranger addressing another stranger. And still, her heart picked up its pace. She shouldn't be entering Everley's private quarters—

But then again, why shouldn't she? This would be her home, too, would it not?

Sooner rather than later.

The thought had her moving into action before she could think it through. Her breathing was coming in gasps now. If only she could slip away long enough to untie her stays. She needed to breathe. She needed—

Thwack!

She'd been rushing so quickly down the darkened hallway she ran headlong into a stranger. A gentleman whose features she couldn't make out and who seemed to be a hunchback or a monster or—

"Ee—" Her strangled screech was cut short by a hand over her mouth. Large, warm, and calloused, it clapped over her mouth so hard her eyes bugged out. And then the form grew.

The shadowy figure grew, and grew, unfolding into a man.

A large man.

A *giant*.

She realized now that he hadn't been a hunchback. He'd been bending over the doorknob of the doorway to her left. She could just make out pins sticking out of the lock before the stranger used his free hand to open the door with a *snick*.

She wanted to scream.

Fear had her immobile.

And then she was moving, but not of her own free will. With a rough grip, the burglar grabbed her by the arms and shoved her into the room.

She was drowning in the darkness. Her earlier feeling of breathlessness growing a millionfold as fear gripped her chest and made her heart pound against her ribcage.

His hand dropped but his low voice was dangerously close to her ear. "Do not scream."

A scream died in her throat.

Not because he told her not to scream. She was just too scared to work her throat properly, that was all.

It wasn't until he took a step back away from her that she remembered how to breathe. "What do you think you're doing?" Her voice was quiet but cold as ice and she was pleased to hear it did not shake.

The man muttered something she could not hear.

"I will give you to the count of three to leave this room, and if you do not, I shall call for help."

The man was moving away from her.

Excellent. She felt a surge of satisfaction just as a match was struck and the dark room gave way to the glow of candlelight.

The gentleman held the candle in one hand as he approached her slowly.

She shuffled back a step. He wasn't running away.

Why was he not running?

Hadn't he understood?

"If my fiancé finds you here—"

"You'll be ruined," he finished.

She gasped in shock. "How *dare* you—"

"A young lady alone in a room with a stranger?" His low voice held a note of amusement that had her hands clenching at her sides. He sounded so casual, talking about her potential ruin as though they were discussing the weather.

And as though this was *her* fault, no less.

"I merely went off in search of a respite," she said. Some of her normal composure was returning rapidly in the face of this stranger's audacity. "*You* were the one sneaking around in the darkened hallways of...of my *fiancé's* home."

The word felt awkward on her tongue, like she'd taken too big of a spoonful of porridge.

His expression was impossible to read in the dim lighting, but she was nearly certain she'd felt him still at that word.

Her chin went up. The power had once again shifted back to her, and they both knew it.

"Fiancé," he murmured. "So then you are..."

"Miss Delilah Clemmons," she finished primly.

"Ah."

She blinked, her eyes narrowing as though that might help her see past the candle's glow to the shadowy figure behind it. His 'ah' said nothing...and everything. It was entirely too knowing for her liking. *What does that mean?* She itched to ask. But admitting to her curiosity would be handing over what little control she had, and that was unthinkable.

Her hands clasped neatly before her, she took a step toward the door. "Yes, well, now that we understand one another," she started, pointedly ignoring the sound of her pounding heart.

"Do not leave just yet, Miss Clemmons." His voice was low, soft...*dangerous*.

She should have been afraid. Distantly she was aware of this. And perhaps she *was*—just a bit—but more than that she was...

Well, she could not say what emotion had her pulse

pounding and her breath finally coming in large gulps as though she'd finally found the oxygen in this house.

Perhaps she was...*exhilarated*.

She pursed her lips. Well, that would not do. She should definitely not be excited by this. "Is that an order?" she said. With a sniff she turned toward the door and reached for the handle. "I do not know who you think you are, sir, but—"

He moved so quickly she found herself blinking in surprise as the door clicked shut just as she'd opened it.

And now he was next to her. So close she could smell his scent—a mix of leather and cologne, and perhaps some sort of spirit. She could see his attire, too. Barely, but enough to make out the fine clothing of a gentleman. Despite the hulking width of his shoulders and his towering frame, he was a gentleman.

A guest.

A guest in her fiancé's home. Soon to be *her* home.

She swallowed down the bitter taste in her mouth. One day soon she'd come to grips with her new reality. "If I scream, it will be your word against mine," she said, once again delighted by how even her voice was.

No one would guess that her heart was fluttering in her chest like a butterfly.

Again—not out of fear. Which made some distant part of her brain wonder about her sanity. Being locked in a room with a giant stranger with a low growl for a voice...

She really ought to be afraid.

Funny, how knowing that did nothing to help this growing sense of...*excitement*.

Yes, there was no denying it now. She had the same surge of energy she used to get as a child before racing her mare across the meadows on the far edge of their country estate.

"Do not scream," he said softly.

She peered up at the man, wishing she could see his eyes,

but only catching glimpses of a nose, a jawline, a twist of his lips as his face flickered in and out of shadows. "I do wish you'd stop telling me what to do, Mister..." She trailed off, waiting for him to fill in the silence.

He did not.

His voice had that irritating note of amusement again when he next spoke. "And I wish you'd stop behaving like a bloody princess and listen to what I have to say."

Her lips parted on a gasp at his language. "I will not—"

"Just listen," he said, and this time it was his exasperation that got through to her.

After all, murders and thieves weren't exasperated, now were they? He could have gone into a rage, but all she'd gotten was a huff of irritation because she wasn't fainting with fear.

And she never would, she decided as she crossed her arms and stared him down.

At least, she hoped she was staring him down. She aimed her gaze in the general direction of his eyes, anyway.

"I am here to protect you," he said.

The words filled the air and hit her ears, but it took a heartbeat for them to register. When they did, she burst out in a laugh that startled her nearly as much as him. "Protect me?" she echoed, an alarming note of hysteria lacing her words. "From what? An intruder? A stranger in a dark room, perhaps?"

She heard his exhale again as she moved toward the door. Other than shoving her into the room, this man hadn't touched her and she'd let that fact make her feel safe.

Safer than it ought.

One of his arms came around her waist and pulled her back away from the door like she weighed nothing.

Then, only then, did she finally think about screaming. In earnest, not just threatening to do it. The hand with the candle hovered before her, temporarily blinding her. She could feel his chest against her back, his breath against her temple as he muttered a curse she'd never heard before.

She should scream. She really ought to scream. "Just what do you think you are doing?"

It was not a scream. It wasn't even as indignant as it ought to have been. It sounded like a prim and proper debutante asking about the weather.

She licked her lips and tried again. "Unhand me at once."

There. Now she'd sounded like the princess he'd accused her of being before.

His husky chuckle sent a thrill down her spine. No, not a thrill. A chill. A chill of *horror*, obviously. There was no other explanation for it.

The silence that followed was amplified by the thudding of her heart. All she could hear was his breath, her heart, and very distantly—as though from another lifetime—the sound of music and laughter as the guests celebrated her engagement.

To a man she'd met once.

And she didn't quite remember it, to be honest.

"There are things you need to know about the man you mean to marry," he said.

"Oh yes?" It came out as a breath. How could she breathe properly when this strange man still had an arm wrapped firmly about her waist? "And what is that?"

"He is not what he seems," the man murmured.

Lord Evil. The nickname rang in her ears and she scowled. Silly Louisa. It was *her* fault she harbored even the tiniest of doubts about his character. He'd never done anything really wrong, of that she was certain. For if he had he would not be celebrated by all the *ton* at this particular moment, now would he? The thought heartened her.

"You do not know him," he said. "Lord Everley is—"

"Pardon me, but this is the man I am to marry." Her tone conveyed nothing but disdain. "There is nothing you can say that will make a difference to me," she said, her nose tilting upward as it was wont to do when she was lying.

He likely *did* know things about her betrothed. A good many things. Things she might not wish to hear...

But what good would that do her? Everley was the man she was to marry. Hearing rumors about his foul deeds wouldn't change that. This was precisely why she'd been avoiding Louisa and Addie.

Prudence too, but mostly because Pru would ask her questions she did not wish to answer.

But the other two—they would wish to tell her things. False things. Hypothetical things.

She tugged against the arm that held her, but she might as well have been battling a stone wall. She grunted in irritation as her brief struggle only succeeded in making his grip tighten to the point that she could not easily breathe.

She'd been struggling to breathe all night, but this had less to do with crippling fear and tight stays, and everything to do with the forearm that was now lodged firmly beneath her ribs. "I need air," she said.

Instantly his grip loosened, and if she'd been quicker—if she'd been afraid the way she ought to be—she would have used that opportunity to fight her way out of his embrace.

As it was, she found herself resting against his chest as she took a deep, calming breath.

His chest was so broad, so firm, so secure, so...*sculpted*—she might have been resting on her own personal throne.

"Better?"

She could feel his chest vibrate against her with that word.

She nodded.

She was better, oddly enough. While reason dictated that

she should be afraid for her very life, she found that she was rather content just now. His embrace was warm and strong and...comforting.

It was also highly improper.

"Do you know, if anyone were to walk in and find us like this, you'll be in just as much trouble as me," she mused.

His laugh was quiet and...nice. "I had considered that, yes."

4

Rupert hadn't just considered this fact. It had been on his mind from the moment he'd dragged her unceremoniously into this room.

If he got caught in Everley's office, it would mean trouble. But if he got caught with Everley's bride-to-be...?

What am I doing? The question echoed in his mind like a gong.

What on earth was he doing?

His mission tonight had been simple. Slip inside this opulent ball and search Everley's office. Everley was too smart to leave incriminating evidence lying about, but he might have found *some* clue, something to point him in the right direction. A sliver of a clue that might help him pick up his old investigation, which had grown cold and fruitless years ago.

But things were different now.

Everley had grown comfortable. He'd even gone and gotten himself *engaged*, for heaven's sake. Surely that was a sign that Everley's heightened state of paranoia and careful precision were faltering. After all, he was letting *this* little minx into his life.

Into his *house*...

The little minx in question shifted against him. "You must surely understand that it would be best for both of us if you let me go at once."

He stared down at the top of her head. From this point of view, all he could make out was dark curls and the pale glow of a high cheekbone but he'd seen enough earlier in the glow of the candlelight.

The girl was a beauty. A diamond of the first water. She could have had her pick of husbands, so how had she ended up with a cruel soul like Everley?

The answer was obvious, of course. Her father had arranged it. Either the old curmudgeon didn't know the extent of Everley's cruel nature or he didn't care. Knowing the two gentlemen involved, he knew without a doubt that this was a business arrangement. Somehow they were both profiting from the merger.

But how?

And at whose expense?

He dipped his head slightly and caught another tantalizing whiff of the scent that had been driving him crazy from the moment he'd first held her close. She smelled of citrus and honey, with a hint of vanilla. A heady blend of sweet and tart that seemed to have entered his system and demand that he take more.

A man could grow addicted to this scent...to the feel of her in his arms...

Oh yes, Everley had found himself a most enticing bride. She would be the perfect addition to this world he was building for himself. The pretty princess on his arm. The smiling, perfect little doll to be pulled out for societal functions and placed back on her shelf when no longer needed.

Poor girl. Did this regal little thing have any idea of what life held in store for her?

He guessed not. Despite her air of confidence and her haughty, imperious tone...he sensed a vulnerability there that she could not quite hide. Not from him. Not when he held her close like this. Not when he could feel her heart beating wildly against its cage.

Her voice grew cold and hard. "I am *waiting*."

Rupert grinned. He couldn't help it. Despite this precarious position, or maybe because of it—he found himself delightfully amused. How long had it been since someone had amused him so?

After so many years working to uncover the secrets of the elite, he'd spent more tedious evenings than he could count with members of the *ton*. He'd spent even more with lowlifes and the downtrodden of society as he unearthed secrets and ferreted out the truth.

But in all that time, he was rarely shocked. Not by people, at least. Their secrets might differ, their circumstances might change, but people tended to be utterly predictable.

This girl?

She was anything but.

He'd expected her to scream, to faint, to burst into hysterics. Instead, she'd been the epitome of arrogance and disdain —on the surface, at least. Beyond that, he suspected, though he could not be certain...

He thought perhaps she was enjoying herself.

Not entirely, clearly, but she wasn't afraid, either. And that was so baffling it made him wish to know her better. To figure out what made her angry, what made her scared...

What made her passionate.

"You are not afraid?" He cursed himself for the words as soon as they were out. Of all the things they ought to discuss, and he chose *this* moment to cater to his curiosity.

She scoffed.

The girl *scoffed*. She was being held against her will by a person she did not know, and she scoffed in disdain at the implication that she might be frightened.

"It is hardly as though we in some back alley, and you are clearly no ruffian," she said. "Why should I be afraid?"

He pulled his head back to try and see her better, marveling a bit at her curious mix of confidence and naiveté. "Do you really believe that bad things can only happen in back alleys?" His voice lowered gruffly as the urge to protect her sweet innocence had him pulling her back against him once more. "Do you think villains cannot be found in high society? Have you not yet learned that men of means and power can make the most fearsome foe?"

She stilled in his arms and he thought perhaps he'd finally gotten through to her the serious nature of his business here. When she moved, it was not to pull away, but to turn in his arms so she was facing him. The candle hovered between them and this close—he was certain she had a full view of his face just as he could see hers.

Beautiful.

She was so much more beautiful than he'd realized. This close he could see her perfection. She was indeed like a doll—all porcelain skin and sharp angles. Her dark hair, brows, and eyes highlighted her fairness and her lips looked rosy and pink even in this light.

But that was where the doll comparison came to an end.

This girl was *life*.

Her eyes glinted with it, and it made her whole body vibrate. Her skin fairly crackled with her energy, her vivacity... her *passion*.

And she was to be wed to Everley.

A rage like he'd never known had him gripping her tightly. Too tightly. With her turned the way she was, she was now pressed against him in an embrace that was so highly inappropriate, it did not bear mentioning.

"Your future husband is just that," he said, his gaze never wavering from her steady glare. "He is a villain of the worst order."

It was there and gone so fast he nearly missed it. A flicker of alarm. She covered it quickly with pursed lips and a haughty sniff. "And I suppose you have some evidence to support this claim?"

Her tone was full of derision, but he knew better. He knew *her* better, though he could never explain how. She was digging for information.

He opened his mouth and shut it, trying to weigh his options. A big part of him wanted to spill all his secrets, to tell her of his past and his suspicions...

When he didn't immediately respond, her lips pressed together in a look of annoyance, that might have been intimidating were she not being held his captive. As it were, it was rather...adorable.

His prisoner was put out, and that made him want to laugh all over again.

"I suppose that is why you are here," she said, her gaze darting to the right and left pointedly. "You are trying to prove whatever claims you have against my...my fiancé."

It was the second time she'd stumbled over the word. He wondered if she knew it.

He wondered if she hated the word as much as he did.

"You are correct," he admitted. "I am here in the hopes of proving my suspicions."

She tugged back, and this time he let her go. Mostly. He kept his arm around her loosely just in case she got the idea to run.

He had no time to battle this girl and whomever came running.

"I knew it," she said, her chin tilting up so her nose was in the air. She looked like a spoiled child, and yet he knew...he knew without a doubt that she was covering up her own fears.

The proud girl would sniff and look down her nose even if a pistol were aimed at her head. He knew this like he knew his own name.

"Aren't you curious?" he asked. "Don't you wish to know what crimes I suspect your betrothed of committing?"

She pursed her lips as she seemed to consider that. "I suppose you wish to tell me."

He felt his lips quirking up against his will. Stubborn little minx. She wouldn't admit to it, but he could see the curiosity in her. "I suspect that he murdered my cousin."

Her eyes widened at his blunt words.

"M-murder? Y-your...*what*?"

He leaned in closer, needing her to hear. To understand. "I don't mean to scare you, Miss Clemmons, but—"

"Well, you're not doing a good job then, are you?" she snapped. Her brows had drawn together and he saw her chest rise and fall as her breathing grew ragged. "You cannot just throw out words like murder. It is just not done."

He growled as he drew her closer, setting the candle on the table so he could use that hand to cup her face in his palm. It was improper, it was intimate—but he was running out of time and patience, and like it or not, he needed this woman to understand what she was getting herself into.

"I don't have the evidence to prove it," he said. "But I know what happened. What's more, I've been watching Everley for years. I've seen the trail of victims he's left in his wake to make him the wealthy, powerful gentleman he is today."

She blinked up at him, her gaze trying to search his in this dark, shadowy room. "If that is true, then why have you done nothing."

"I have never been able to prove my suspicions—"

"So why *now*?" Her voice was rising, imperious even when upset. His gaze shot to the door. If she kept talking loudly, someone could hear. Aside from that, he knew for a fact that Everley often conducted business in his office during his parties. He was known for using his social gatherings to do his dirty work—extortion, blackmail, and yes—murder.

"Why are you here now?" she continued. "At my engagement party, no less."

"Keep your voice down," he murmured. "Unless you wish us to be caught and your reputation to be ruined."

She narrowed her eyes and made a noise he'd call a growl if it had come from a man. As it was it was a little more high-pitched, and entirely too enticing. "Don't you threaten me at my own party, and in my own home." She blinked rapidly and gave her head a little shake. "It *will* be my home," she continued, but now he wasn't entirely certain if she were reminding him or herself.

"I didn't come here to scare you," he said. "I came here to save you."

She stared at him for a long moment, her lips parting with surprise.

His gaze dropped to those lips.

He wanted to kiss her.

The realization struck him upside the head and left him reeling. He was a professional. He never got distracted whilst on a mission, and most certainly not while in the midst of rifling through the office of his arch nemesis. And yet, here he was. Staring at those lush lips and imagining what it might be like to press his lips to hers. What sort of sound she would make, how heatedly she would respond...

"You...are here to save me." Her voice hitched in the middle and he couldn't tell if she were fighting a sob or a laugh.

"You...you..." She let out a choked laugh. "*You* are here to save *me*." She gave her head a little shake and seemed to remember herself, pushing against his chest hard to take a step away. Her shoulders pushed back and her head went high. "I have no need of saving, Mister..." She arched a brow.

"Calloway," he finished. A twinge of guilt flickered in his gut, but he pushed it aside. He owed this girl nothing, certainly not the whole unvarnished truth. And besides, it wasn't a lie. Mr. Rupert Calloway was the name he'd been using for years now, having eschewed the honorary title that was his right. Titles were all well and good, and having one certainly served its purpose from time to time, but in his line of work, being a Mr. Nobody-in-Particular seemed best.

Her lips curved into a sneer. "Mr. Calloway," she repeated, as though engraving it to her memory. "You seem to forget that *I* am the one that belongs here. And if my future husband is as ruthless as you claim, surely it is *you* who needs saving." She took her time before adding, "By me."

He nearly laughed at her arrogant confidence. He might have if he wasn't so worried for her safety. He'd been concerned for her when she was just a name, an acquaintance of an old friend. But now he *feared* for her. Because she was...

Well, because she was *her*.

A weak woman might be able to exist at Everley's side. A woman less stubborn, less determined, less strong-willed, less...

Perfect.

No, not perfect. A woman less *infuriating*. That was the word he'd been looking for. A woman less infuriating might be able to turn a blind eye to her husband's wicked ways, and perhaps survive being wedded to Everley in some sort of ignorant bliss.

But someone like Delilah... She was not simple, she was not easy, and she would definitely be a thorn in Everley's side.

And Everley would have no problem getting rid of her if she were problematic. That thought left Rupert shaking with rage. "Listen to me, Delilah—" His use of her given name had her eyes widening in surprise but he ignored it. "You need to take this seriously."

"Oh, I do," she cut in.

He could practically see the walls she was constructing around her, protecting herself, withdrawing into the picture of feminine grace and charm.

Shutting him out, in the process.

"I think I understand quite well," she said. "You wish to destroy my husband."

He flinched at her use of that word. He would kill Everley first before he ever let him get his hands on this woman.

For a man who prided himself on his even-keeled nature, he barely recognized what was happening to him. This was an investigation. One that had personal ties to him, yes, but it was still his work. His mission.

He couldn't let his emotions get involved.

Not again.

That was how Everley had bested him the last time. And he'd sworn he wouldn't let that happen again.

"You didn't deny it," she said.

He hadn't. How could he? He wished for nothing less than the complete ruin of Lord Everley.

"Which means," she said slowly. "You wish to destroy me, as well."

His brows drew down as he took a step toward her. If she'd retreated, he might have stopped. But she didn't. This foolish girl was too stubborn for her own good. So invested in her bravado that she'd leap headlong into this match out of sheer spite, he had no doubt. "Now look here, Delilah."

"It is Miss Clemmons to you," she said pertly, her head tilted back so she could maintain eye contact. "Soon to be

Lady Everley." She took a step back, but not out of fear from his towering height—no, her step was regal and controlled as she gestured toward the door. "I believe we are done here."

"But you do not—"

"I said, we are through." Her mouth grew pinched and he hated it. Such a shame to lose those beautiful lush lips to an expression like that. Like she'd just sucked on a lemon.

She was waiting with her hand raised, along with her chin. She looked every inch a lady. She'd fit the role of baroness perfectly—in physicality, at least.

Were she marrying any other gentleman he might have even admired her loyalty and her courage.

Eyeing her now, he knew she had made up her mind. It didn't take a fully lit room to see the stubborn set of her jaw or the hard determination in her eyes.

His mind raced to think of any logic she might listen to. He thought of telling her that Tolston had sent him but dismissed it. He wouldn't put it past her to tell her husband-to-be about the stranger lurking in his halls. Perhaps even tell him the details of this conversation.

He could not risk putting his friend's reputation on the line or have Everley turn his dastardly efforts against the good earl.

He could think of no argument other than the one he'd given, and that had not been enough for this stubborn little fool.

They both tensed at the sound of voices coming down the hallway, staring at the door until the booming laughter passed, along with a woman's higher-pitched laugh.

When the threat was over, he turned to see her staring at him. Studying him. Even in this light, she seemed to see it all—his thick brows, the wide jaw, the flat nose—every facet of his face, which friends called rugged and foes called menacing. Despite his noble lineage, he'd been graced with the appearance of those same back-alley thieves Miss Clemmons thought fit to fear.

He waited for her judgement, but if she passed any, he could not see it. The only gesture that gave away her thoughts was the frown that touched her lips as she eyed his hair which was unfashionably long where it brushed against his collar. The fine clothes he'd scrounged up from the back of his wardrobe, but by the time he'd realized he'd let himself go recently—it had been too late to do much for his appearance other than a quick shave.

"Why are you here now?" she asked.

"I beg your pardon?" It wasn't often he was called upon to play dumb, and he wasn't certain it did him credit.

The way she cocked one eyebrow told him she wasn't fooled. "Why now? You said you've been investigating Everley, but why are you here now, risking your very life to find new evidence."

He let out a huff of amusement. "I wouldn't say I was risking my life."

She arched both brows now. "I would. You said yourself that Everley is capable of murder, and yet here you are. Breaking into his private quarters, kidnapping his fiancée—"

"Kidnapping?" he interjected.

She ignored the protest. "Why *now*?"

She wasn't going to let this go, but he could see her suspicion grow. A part of her, at least, was wondering if this was connected to her.

Smart girl.

Smart but foolish if she thought she was immune from Everley's cruelty because she was to be his wife.

Voices echoed outside the door again, this time it was male voices and they were talking. "I had better go." He looked around but before he could figure out his best chance of escape she pointed behind him.

"That window. The drop isn't too far."

He arched his brows in surprise and she shrugged. "A friend might have told me."

He wanted to ask her to elaborate but time was running out. He glanced around the office with a frustrated growl. After all these years he'd gotten so close.

Close enough to actually catch the man who'd murdered his best friend.

And he'd lost his chance because he was trying to talk sense into a senseless twit.

She planted her hands on her hips and that was when he realized he'd muttered some of that aloud. "Senseless twit, am I? I am not the one who's trying to snoop around Lord Evil while he's entertaining at his own engagement party."

Lord...*Evil?* He could not have heard her right.

Before he could ask her to explain, she glanced over her shoulder, alerted as he was by the growing volume of those voices. "Go on," she said. "Out with you." And with that she shoved him toward the window.

She stopped when they reached it and he threw up the window. "Just tell me," she said as he began his ungraceful climb out the window. "Why now?"

Because of you. He could not tell her that, though it was clear she suspected. He didn't have to answer at all, but that undeniable intelligence in her eyes told him she would not be satisfied without an answer, and maybe...

Maybe that curiosity would help her to learn the real nature of the man she was wearing. Maybe...

His gaze caught hers when he was halfway out the window.

"What is it?" she asked, clearly reading his tension.

He had to make a decision and he had to make it quick. "Your loving fiancé," he started, enjoying the way her jaw muscle ticked in irritation at the endearment. "One of his many vices is smuggling."

She frowned. "Smuggling?"

"Among other things," he said.

The voices grew louder and he heard Everley's unmistakable laugh—humorless and cold and too loud for any occasion.

"What does that have to do with you. Being here. Tonight." She listed the three things like they were separate entities.

He hovered there, half in and half out of the room, hating that he even noticed how beautiful she was in the glow of the moonlight. Even more beautiful than in the candlelight, and wouldn't have imagine that possible had he not seen it with his own eyes.

She was beautiful—and she knew it. That was the only explanation for her haughty, spoiled arrogance.

"I'm looking for proof," he said. Again, not a total lie. He had been given a hint from one of his friends down at the dock that a shipment was coming in soon. A man like Everley could have stopped with the illegal trades years ago. He no longer needed the money now that he'd acquired a fortune... along with his cousin's title.

But men like Everley never knew when to stop. They always pushed too hard, too far—and Rupert was betting on the fact that he was doing the same thing now. He hadn't given up his criminal ways just because he'd gotten himself a title. If anything, Rupert guessed that Everley had only grown more ambitious given his new status in society.

It was a bet he'd been willing to bet his life on by coming here tonight.

Looking at this little queen standing there in all her regal glory, it occurred to him—she might just be the in he needed.

Wariness crept over him. It was one thing to bet his own

life, quite another to rope a young debutante into helping him.

No. He could not. He *would* not, even though he was certain that all it would take was a challenge. A subtle prick to her pride followed by a not-so-subtle dare...

She'd do his job for him and with ease since she had free reign of this home...or would soon enough.

"What is it?" she demanded. "Why are you looking at me like that?"

"Like what?" He grinned before she could respond. It was rather diverting to make her scowl. Yes, Everley had chosen well. He'd been looking for the belle of the ball and he'd found her.

He'd taken Rupert's best friend to score a title and estate, had nearly taken *his* life when he'd gotten close to catching him, and now...

Rupert took one last look at the enchanting little minx with the upturned nose.

And now Everley had gotten the girl.

Life, as Rupert already well knew, just was not fair.

She planted her hands on her hips, not even turning to look when a hand rattled the doorknob. "Why that look?"

She hated not having all the answers, but she wouldn't get any more from him. He'd do his best to keep her out of this. Whether she liked it or not.

"Do yourself a favor, Princess," he said as his feet landed on the ground and only his eyes peered over the edge. "Stay out of my way. Stay out of his way. And whatever you do, do not cause trouble."

Her eyes widened in outrage. "Do not cause trouble? Says the man who means to ruin my life."

"No, I mean to ruin his. I already told you, it is *you* I hope to save."

That made her furious, which made him feel like laughing.

A real laugh. The kind of laugh he hadn't reveled in for an age.

"Stay safe, Princess," he said as he backed away.

She came closer to keep him in her sights.

"If you need me, I will save you."

She frowned. "How would I find you?" Then, just as quickly, she seemed to remember herself. "Not that I will need your help."

"When you do..." He grinned, despite the circumstances. "*I* will find *you*."

5

I will find *you.*

Conceited man. She scowled at the window even after he disappeared, only spinning around when the door flew open and her fiancé strode in with two men she did not know behind him.

They all stopped short at the sight of her. Everley recovered first. "Delilah. My dear." He strode toward her with a brilliant smile that did not reach his eyes and left her cold. She forced a smile of her own as he approached, and they basically reenacted their first meeting earlier this same evening.

Which was to say, they said all the correct things as onlookers watched. They made pleasantries and pretended to be happy to see one another.

"What are you doing alone in here?" he asked.

As he did, his gaze moved to the open window. She took a step to the left to block his view, gesturing to the window as she did so. "I'm afraid I became overheated." She fluttered her lashes and smiled sweetly. Her stepmother had taught her how to give this look many years ago and it was a skill she called upon often. The look said *soft, sweet...innocent.*

Everley's look said *concerned.* At least, that was what he'd apparently aimed for. His eyes said *curious.* "Are you well or—"

"Oh yes," she said with a little laugh. "I am just not used to such lavish parties, I'm afraid. The crowd became too much."

His smile softened as he took her by the elbow and led her toward the hallway. "That is my fault, my dear. I should have been attending to your needs this evening." He gestured toward the strange men who were watching her with matching fatherly smiles. "I am afraid I have been distracted by business endeavors."

"Oh, please, do not let me interrupt you," she said. "I was meaning to find my friends. I am certain they are wondering where I am."

This, she knew, was very true.

His grip on her arm tightened as he smiled down at her, the sound of music swelling as they drew closer to the center of the action. "I expect they are," he said. "You must not keep them waiting."

She tried to match his smile and faltered. When her gaze met his, her skin crawled. Her stomach sank at the coldness she saw there, barely hidden beneath a smiling façade.

Lord Evil.

Silly nickname. But even as she thought it, Mr. Calloway's accusations were swirling through her mind, making her doubt everything.

Murderer. The word flashed through her mind and she stumbled a bit as she kept pace with her fiancé. When they spotted her friends, gathered together nearby, Lord Everley's grip on her loosened.

Louisa was waving madly as the others openly stared.

"If you'll excuse me," her fiancé said smoothly. "I must

attend to business. Why don't you enjoy some time with your delightful young friends and be sure to save me a dance, hmm?"

He didn't bother to wait for an answer, and Delilah was left to face her friends.

Her very enthusiastic, much too curious friends.

When Miss Grayson gave her a kind smile, she knew there was nothing for it. She might have been able to ignore Louisa, and Addie...even Prudence who was no doubt miserable this evening.

Pru hated crowds and deplored dancing.

But Miss Grayson's kindness was impossible to ignore. Only a beast would snub their teacher by walking past and pretending not to see them.

With a sigh she headed toward her friends who welcomed her warmly.

"At last!" Louisa exclaimed, as though Delilah had been lost at sea.

"We've missed you," Addie said with a smile.

Prudence wore a scowl that Delilah knew well. Her friend tended to be sanctimonious and a bit of a mother hen, but when all was said and done, Prudence had a big heart. Perhaps too big. She worried far too much about those she loved, and Delilah—for reasons still unbeknownst to her— was on that list.

She gave Prudence what she hoped was a reassuring smile before turning to Miss Grayson. Always kind, forever graceful, Miss Grayson was that sad example of a lovely young lady who was bound to be a spinster because of reasons outside her purview. Miss Grayson's smile was gentle and understanding. "You have been missed," she said, her eyes warm with amusement as Louisa chose that moment to launch into a round of questions that would never be answered.

Addie stepped in once more to temper her friend's loud

questions about why she was marrying Lord Evil, and why she hadn't been back to the house to see them.

"As you can see, we've been curious to hear the details of your engagement," Addie said mildly.

Delilah rolled her eyes at the understatement just as the first notes of a waltz began to play.

"Were you kidnapped?" Louisa hissed in a loud whisper.

"What?" Delilah laughed. "Of course not, silly." Her gaze never quite focused on any one of them as she looked around. "I have been busy, that's all. Planning a wedding on such short notice has taken up all my time, I'm afraid."

Her response was met by silence all around.

Luckily, Delilah was saved by two smitten gentlemen. Lord Tolston and Lord Tumberland joined their group to claim their fiancées for a dance. "We will be back," Louisa said as her future husband dragged her away toward the dance floor.

Delilah watched with a jolt of disgust as the two couples went off with nauseatingly sweet smiles and soft laughter that spoke of private jokes and happy plans.

"Love matches," Prudence said with a weary sigh before her. "Is there anything more sickening?"

Miss Grayson laughed lightly, opting to take Prudence's comment as a joke, though Delilah knew it was not.

"If you'll excuse me," Miss Grayson said, looking from Delilah to Prudence. "I believe I see an old acquaintance." She fooled no one. Miss Grayson was hoping to give Delilah and her closest friend a moment alone, and Delilah hated her for it.

She did not wish to answer questions, not when her heart was still pounding from that run-in with a burglar. Not when her mind still raced with questions after hearing his accusations.

Miss Grayson leaned toward her. "We are all relieved to

see you safe and well," she said. "You know you are always welcome at the school...for any reason." She hitched her brows slightly. "We all care about you, and we are here if you need us."

Delilah nodded, her throat temporary choked with emotion as she watched Miss Grayson walk away.

"Well," Prudence said with a sigh. "I suppose you're pleased."

Delilah stiffened at her friend's casual remark. "Pleased?"

Her friend shot her a sidelong look. "You're about to marry a man as rich as Midas. Isn't that what you've always dreamt of?"

"It was what I was born to do," she quipped, her tone filled with a bravado that made Prudence laugh, as she'd hoped. This was an old joke of theirs. From the first day they'd met at the school, Pru was the one to see that not all of Delilah's snobbery was genuine.

Some of it was...just not all.

"Yes, yes," Pru said. "You were born to be a queen."

Delilah's smile felt more forced than ever since it was aimed at a friend. Perhaps not born to be a queen, but raised to be a trophy. From the moment she could walk, she'd understood that her sole purpose in life, in her family, was to marry well.

It had always been her dream.

Her father's dream.

It had been both of their dream. It was all she was good for, and everyone knew that.

She sighed as a sort of lethargic weariness stole over her. The energy that had been coursing through her after that bizarre encounter was starting to fade, leaving her limbs weighted and her mind foggy with exhaustion.

Pru shot her a sidelong look. "What's wrong?" she demanded.

"Pardon me?"

Pru's lips pursed and her expression said 'don't even try to fool me.' "You sighed just now as though you'd just ruined your best gown."

"Did I?" she murmured.

Pru turned to face her. "Are you going to tell me what's happened?" When she didn't immediately respond, she continued. "Are you going to tell me why you're suddenly betrothed to Lord Evil?"

"Hush," she said quickly, peeking around to see who might have heard. "I do wish you all would stop using that name." She arched her brows. "I understand Louisa and Addie saying it as a joke, but that sort of immaturity is beneath you, Prudence."

Prudence just stared at her evenly, scrutinizing her expression. "What is going on, Dee?"

Oh nothing. I've just been alone with an overbearing oaf who believes my fiancé to be a murderer and a smuggler.

She frowned. It was the smuggler bit that had gotten to her. Murderer? The very accusation had felt too far-fetched. Murderers did not exist amongst the *ton*. He might have been a bit fearsome, but really…accusing Lord Everley of murder had just been melodrama on Mr. Calloway's part.

That man ought to be the one engaged to Louisa, not the proper, practical Lord Tumberland.

The thought of the stranger and Louisa made her inexplicably angry.

"Delilah, do try and smile," Prudence murmured. "You look like an evil queen from a fairy tale, ready to smite the townspeople."

Delilah blinked and looked around to see that indeed she had been garnering some stares from passersby. She plastered a small smile on her face and lifted her chin.

"You know we all have questions," Pru started again.

"Why do you think I haven't returned to the school?" she returned.

Pru huffed. "We're just worried about you."

"You have nothing to fear." Delilah's voice was pleasingly cool, wonderfully collected. "I was born and raised to marry someone of great fortune. My father has chosen Lord Everley."

"And you are all right with that," Prudence said, doubt clear in her voice.

"Of course. Why wouldn't I be?"

"Addie said—"

Delilah waved aside the protest. "Oh please. Addie is nearly as dramatic as Louisa, and of course she was beside herself when her brother was in danger. Can we really trust her word on the matter?"

Delilah didn't have to look over to know Prudence was scowling at her. "Do you really believe that? Do you truly believe you have nothing to fear or do you just not want to admit that you might be wrong?"

Delilah opened her mouth to verbally smack down her friend but no words came out. She blamed it on the strange encounter back in Everley's office.

Of course she'd been rattled by a run-in with a burglar. The thought of his large frame behind her, holding her tight… She shivered, but not from fear.

"Are you all right?"

Delilah huffed. "I wish people would stop asking me that. What will it take to prove that I am fine?"

Prudence was silent for too long before turning to face the dance floor with a sigh. "I do not know, Dee. What will it take for *you* to believe that?"

She shot her friend a glare. She hated when Pru got all high and mighty on her like this.

She hated it even more when Pru was right.

She'd been in a fog of disbelief these past two weeks as she let her stepmother arrange the wedding, and avoided seeing the people who might make her doubt her new future.

Delilah sniffed as she watched Addie and Tolston smiling at one another like lovesick fools. Louisa and Tumberland had already left the dance floor and were headed toward the balcony.

She had never expected a love match, and as such had never hoped for one. Why dream of something one cannot have? It would only lead to disappointment. She'd always known the day would come when she would marry a man who did not fit any girlish dream for a husband.

She ought to be grateful that Everley wasn't old enough to be her grandfather, or so overweight he could hardly move, or so unattractive he made women flee the room.

No, as far as all that went, she was quite lucky. As far as looks and age went, her fiancé was better than she'd expected.

But his character...?

She found her gaze flitting back toward the hallway. He had not yet reappeared. What *was* his business, exactly?

Was she allowed to ask?

It was Prudence's question that clung to her now and made her mind race. What *would* put her at ease?

She knew better than to trust Addie and Louisa's suspicions, and she shouldn't let some stranger's accusations get to her either.

But they had.

Mr. Calloway's words and his voice and his touch. Everything about him had gotten to her. The whole experience had rattled her. It had shaken her out of her fog. And now, despite her best efforts, she couldn't go back. His grin just before he'd disappeared from view haunted her.

Stupid, arrogant man.

His attitude was one of challenge, and she had always risen to a challenge.

So, he thought she needed saving? She would see about that.

"You have a look about you, Dee..." Prudence was watching her closely.

"Oh yes?" she asked mildly. "And what look is that?"

"It's very similar to the look Louisa gets when she's about to stir up trouble."

Delilah gave a huff of indignation. "I am nothing like Louisa. I do not seek out mischief."

But she *did* seek out the truth. She'd never been one to sit by meekly and watch her life unfold, and she certainly wouldn't start now.

She had no idea what his murder allegations were about—likely a duel gone wrong, or something to that effect. It was the smuggling charge that stuck with her and made her uneasy. Such an odd thing to accuse a gentleman like Lord Everley of, particularly without proof.

She pursed her lips as she glanced toward the hallway. Of course, that was likely why he was here. Looking for proof.

An idea took root and began to grow.

"Oh yes, you definitely look like Louisa right now," Prudence said quietly beside her.

Delilah shushed her halfheartedly. This wasn't mischief or mere curiosity. This was her duty...to Everley. She'd seek out the proof that the burglar was seeking, and when she failed to find it, she would know it with certainty.

She could put her own mind to rest and if she ever had the misfortune of running into Mr. Calloway again she would be able to put him soundly in his place.

She smiled.

"I'm worried about you," Prudence said when she'd turned back to face her friend.

"Don't be," she said. "I've never felt better."

This, she realized, was the truth. Despite the startling events of this evening, or perhaps because of them...she had a mission. An agenda.

She had a *challenge*.

For the first time in weeks, she was beginning to feel like herself again.

6

Delilah's smile never faltered as she confronted her stepmother in the family's drawing room. "Oh, but I should very much like to join you."

Her stepmother stared at her, her eyes blank as always. She likely hadn't expected a battle, not after Delilah had sat by so meekly throughout wedding plans to date. But today everything was different.

"Very well. If you wish it," the baroness said.

"I do." Delilah followed her stepmother to the waiting carriage and they made their way together to Everley's townhouse in Mayfair.

The air smelled of rotting flowers as the unseasonable heat crept over the city, and Delilah did her best not to take it as a sign that the world seemed to have been burning with the flames of hell from the moment she'd agreed to marry the devil.

Lord Everley.

She pressed her lips together in annoyance at her own imagination. She was here to prove that Louisa, Addie, and most definitely that stranger had gotten it all wrong. Surely her fiancé wasn't so bad as he was made out to be.

Right?

The nagging worry would be allayed as well once she'd cleared her mind of their dramatic notions.

Everley greeted them warmly and some of her apprehensions faded even further at the attention he paid to her and her stepmother. His manners were impeccable.

Smugglers surely did not have impeccable manners. Murderers, perhaps, but not common criminals.

She smiled beatifically over tea, she answered his enquiries as to her health and her experience at the engagement ball with pleasure. See? This was a man she ought to be proud to marry. This was the man her father had chosen for her—from his sickbed, of course, but she was certain he'd done his due diligence.

He would hardly hand her over to a *murderer*.

She sipped her tea and worked herself into a righteous anger over the matter. Her husband-to-be was being unfairly persecuted and it was up to her to make this right.

She imagined the look on that brute Mr. Calloway's face when she slapped him across the face with her evidence. Or her *lack* of evidence.

Either way, she would show him who needed saving. And it wasn't her.

Delilah Clemmons needed no help from anyone. Even less so once she was secure in a marriage to a man as wealthy as a king. Then she'd have power. She'd like to see Mr. Calloway try to talk to tell her she was a helpless princess then. *Hmmph.*

"Delilah?" Her stepmother eyed her oddly and Delilah realized she hadn't been paying attention.

"Yes? What? Er...Pardon me." She set her teacup down.

Her stepmother's smile was placid. Cool. Her father had

married the epitome of grace and beauty in the hopes that she would be a good role model for Delilah. Growing up she'd often wished her father had focused more on finding her a mother figure rather than a role model, but perhaps the two were one in the same in some cases.

Not in theirs.

Though at this precise moment, her stepmother was doing an excellent job of feigning motherly concern. "Would you like to rest a bit, dear?" She glanced over at Lord Everley who wore matching look of beneficence. "Lord Everley and I can certainly handle matters from here."

Delilah wanted to protest. This was her wedding, her honeymoon…her future they were discussing. If anyone should take part in these conversations it was she.

And since when had these two become such close friends?

But all that was beside the point because this served her purposes quite nicely. Her stepmother had neatly handed her the excuse she needed. "Do you know, this weather does have me feeling a bit piqued," she said with a flutter of her lashes. "If you both wouldn't mind…"

"Of course not!" Everley was beckoning to a servant to attend to her. "We must keep you in good health for the big day, mustn't we?"

She returned his smile evenly, trying not to note the excessively paternal note in his voice. It was nice that he was looking after her welfare.

It was hardly necessary, of course, but perhaps he was used to dealing with women of less solid constitutions.

"Henderson will take you to the sun room. You shall be quite comfortable there," he said. Turning to the servant, he added, "Be sure to send her tea."

Delilah bit her lip to keep from telling them both that she didn't wish to drink tea. The last thing she wanted was for servants to come and check on her and find her gone.

Something about the look in Everley's eyes stopped her from protesting. It was good manners to accept, anyhow. But the moment she and Henderson were out of view and earshot, she turned to the older man. "I do not require any more tea at the moment. But I will let you know when I do."

"Very good, miss."

And so she found herself in the sun room, which was indeed quite comfortable, and more importantly she found herself alone. Blissfully alone. She took a moment to enjoy the silence, the lack of pretense—and then she made her move.

She crept quickly and quietly through the hallways. She'd done her fair share of exploring the main areas of the first floor on the night of the ball and tonight she navigated them smoothly. She had a lie prepared in the event that she ran into someone, but the lie was unnecessary. Aside from some voices coming from the top of a staircase as she passed, the home was utterly silent.

Perhaps too silent. The ticking of the clock when she reached Everley's office was ominous in the otherwise silent room. The door had been closed but not locked, like it had been the other night.

She'd used extra hair pins in the event that she might need them, but again...her preparations proved unnecessary. The door swung open quietly and she found herself back in the room that had been haunting her dreams and her memories for the last two days.

In the cold light of day, the room looked far more inviting, and without Mr. Calloway ...

Well, without him the room felt *bigger*, at least...and far less exciting.

Not that *he* was exciting. Odds were he was just a lowly bow street runner hired to investigate Everley. Maybe he'd even been hired by Tolston himself. She scowled at the desk as she crossed to it. She'd continued to avoid the school, just as she had for weeks, but now it occurred to her that Addie might have had information on that infernal man who'd held her hostage.

Not that it mattered.

He didn't matter.

She looked around the spacious, bizarrely empty space with a feeling of...well, emptiness. It had seemed so different last time she was here and she supposed she'd been looking forward to this moment because she'd thought she'd recapture that sensation.

The exhilaration. The thrill. The novelty of rising to a challenge, of taking her life in her own hands...

She sighed as she shoved the disappointment aside and focused on the task before her. His desk. There was no better place to start, was there?

A little while later, after carefully rifling through drawers and flipping through his diary, she had to admit that this plan was better in theory than in practicality.

For one thing, she had no idea what she was looking for. If anything, she ought to hope to find nothing, for if he were innocent there would be no incriminating evidence to be found, now would there?

The whole endeavor was starting to feel pointless, really. Maybe even silly. When no red flags reared up—and really, what had she expected to find? A confession of murder? A pirate's flag with Everley's name stamped upon it?

"So daft, Delilah," she sighed in irritation as she shut the last drawer, made a point of ensuring everything looked untouched and then headed toward the hallway.

The door had no sooner clicked shut behind her when Everley and her stepmother came around the corner. They stopped at the sight of her there. Her stepmother did not seem surprised to see her, but then again...her stepmother likely did not know where the sun room was.

Or that Delilah was supposed to be in it.

She met Lord Everley's gaze and it was there and gone in a heartbeat, but she'd seen it. Not anger.

That would imply heat. No, this was something cold as ice.

It was hatred.

Cruelty.

It was...*evil.*

He covered it quickly, but it left her frozen in place, her mouth dry and her limbs trembling from that brief glance. When his eyes moved away from her, she nearly slumped over in relief, but his gaze merely moved to his office door and then back to her.

He knows.

He knew exactly what she'd been up to. Her mind teemed with too many thoughts to make any sense at all as her tongue seemed to swell to double its size.

She had no excuse. What was her excuse?

"The library!" The words tumbled out of her too quickly, and far too loud for the narrow chamber. "I was looking for the library."

Her stepmother's brows hitched up in surprise but Everley was once more the picture of hospitality.

"An avid reader, are you?" he said.

"Umm, yes. That's right." She licked her lips. She was lying and they both knew it. She felt ridiculous continuing. But she'd come this far, so she forced herself to add, "I thought it might help me take my mind off the wedding details."

"Ah, I see." His brows drew together and he feigned concern so well, she nearly believed it. "Is the impending wedding causing you distress?"

"No," she said quickly. "It is just...a lot to consider."

He eyed her as though he expected her to continue.

When she did not, he gestured behind him. "You must have gotten turned around then. The library is in the opposite direction."

"Oh! How silly of me." She gave her head a little shake. "It must be this heat."

"Yes," he said, his voice dry and flat. "You do seem under the weather today. Perhaps we ought to send you home."

"That is probably for the best," her stepmother chimed in. "You can take our carriage home, dear. I will send for a hired hack when we are through here."

Alarm shot through Delilah, along with relief. She wanted to be gone, but being dismissed so summarily made her uneasy. Any sense of control she'd been feeling since she'd decided to investigate her own fiancé had withered and died.

Truthfully, it had fled the moment she'd stepped foot in Everley's study and realized...she was alone.

And she had no idea what she was doing.

But here, now, with her mouth gaping as she searched for an excuse to stay. To make this right...

She might as well have been a small child being sent off to bed without supper.

"Nonsense," Everley said with a sickening smile in her stepmother's direction. "I shall have my carriage take you home when you are ready."

She dipped her head in humble thanks, and Delilah had the urge to snap at her. *Charlatan.* Her stepmother had always been the best actress she knew, but she rarely saw it on such flagrant display.

At Miss Grayson's school, Delilah was known for the sting of her tongue, for her sharp retorts and withering comebacks. And yet here, now, in the stifling presence of her stepmother and fiancé, all she could manage was a meek nod of assent as she turned toward the sun room and the library.

"Miss Clemmons." Everley had been calling her Delilah earlier today. She gulped at the change and froze with her back to her future husband. "Do stay in the library until the carriage is brought around, won't you? We wouldn't want you to get lost again."

She nodded quickly, already scurrying away.

7

Rupert tensed in the spot where he hid. She'd been in there forever. What on earth were they doing all day?

Standing guard was never his favorite task when investigating. The long hours of waiting for action, of keeping vigilant watch while hours ticked by...

It was tedious, at best.

But today was worse than most.

She was in there.

His hands clenched and unclenched rhythmically as he fought for calm. It was impossible that Delilah could look any more beautiful in the daylight than she had in the moonlight or the candlelight.

But she had.

Somehow that was infuriating. It wasn't fair that she be quite so beautiful on top of being a spitfire with courage and wit.

It was not fair that Everley had met her first, and it certainly was not right that she was to be his.

He'd already had enough reason to want Everley out of

the picture, but now, with Delilah's future on the line, his plans had grown far more urgent. He could no longer dig into Everley's life from the sidelines.

It was time to face him head on.

When the door to the townhouse opened, he tensed again, ready to lunge into action to follow the girl.

It was a footman, carrying a message, no doubt. Rupert watched him go, and a part of him wished he could follow. If he'd had an accomplice here today he would have sent them off to do just that. But he couldn't be in two places at once, and his priority had to be Delilah. He had to make sure she left here unharmed and that she got home safe. His chest tightened and a feeling he wasn't quite familiar with crept over him.

Was this...fear?

He'd thought he was immune to such things. After spending years courting danger, it took a great deal to rattle his nerves.

But perhaps that was because it had always been his own life in danger. He'd never had an innocent to worry over.

And entitled brat or not, Delilah was an innocent. She was feisty and smart and unbearably haughty...but she was still an innocent.

And she was his to protect.

Her being involved added a new level of complications to his plans. Now it was no longer so clean cut. He couldn't just take Everley down, he had to ensure she didn't get harmed in the process.

And he *would* take Everley down. It was just a matter of time.

His informant at the docks seemed to think a shipment would be coming soon. Unfortunately his informant wasn't close enough to Everley's men to know any of the details.

Little things like which day and what time.

Frustration had him growling as he moved his neck to ease some of the tension building there.

All afternoon she'd been in there, and now the sun was starting to set. Twilight was setting in and the gray overcast day made it feel later than it was.

And then...sunshine appeared.

He scoffed at his own stupidity as soon as the thought occurred, but there she was. Delilah, looking like a ray of sunshine on this cloudy day as she finally appeared on the steps of the townhouse.

Everley and her stepmother were beside her as the carriage rolled to a stop in front of them.

He watched Delilah climb in and waited for her stepmother to follow, but the perfectly put together blonde took a step back instead as the carriage door was shut.

Delilah was alone.

He eyed the carriage's departure and Everley's retreat into his home. Rupert did not even have to stop to decide where his loyalties lie. The moment the door shut behind the stepmother, he was on his horse and following the carriage.

He had an idea where Delilah's family lived, and so it was with no small amount of alarm that he watched the carriage take a wrong turn. And then another.

They were heading through a neighborhood where a lady like Delilah should never visit, even if she were not alone and unprotected. Ice ran through his veins as he watched the inevitable, as though he'd read the novel and knew each player's move before it occurred.

Sure enough, the carriage came to a stop just as a group of rogues stepped out of the shadows.

One of them threw open the door, but he did not hear Delilah scream.

But then, she *wouldn't* give the knaves that satisfaction.

The driver was long gone by the time Rupert was on top

of them, off his horse and throwing punches, his elbow colliding with a jaw before spinning to tear the rogue in the carriage door out of the way.

Delilah cowered in the corner, her face pale as she scrambled back as far as she could go when he entered.

"Get out of here you—you—" Her voice trailed off as her eyes widened in surprise.

"Hello, love," he said, managing a grin to put her at ease as he reached for her hand. "I'm afraid I'll need you to come with me."

She blinked once and then she moved into action, following his lead and not even feigning dismay when he tossed her unceremoniously atop his horse.

The vagabonds had scattered.

They likely weren't getting paid enough to take a beating. Just to harm an innocent.

Rage had always helped him focus, and right now his whole world came down to one thing. One *person*.

Delilah.

He had to keep her safe.

Leaping up so he was seated behind her, he urged the horse into action, leaving the carriage where it was in the midst of a bad neighborhood, as onlookers peered out of dingy windows at the commotion.

Neither of them spoke as he rode back toward his home. He helped her down, handing the horse over to a groomsman as he led her inside.

She was quiet.

Too quiet.

He watched her carefully as he instructed a servant to bring refreshments to the parlor, the only room that was lit since he hadn't been expecting guests.

It wasn't until the door to the parlor shut behind them that she seemed to come to life.

"Where have you brought me?" Her voice was too high and far sharper than he'd expected.

"To my home."

She huffed. "This is entirely improper."

He stared at her in surprise...and possibly some amusement, though he didn't wish to admit it. He really should not be laughing at a helpless victim.

And if she were to ever act helpless, he would certainly not be fighting laughter. "Would you have preferred that I wait for a chaperone before rescuing you?" he asked mildly.

She blinked and turned to stare at a portrait on the wall. "You live here?"

He looked around as if he might find a friend with whom he could commiserate. He'd brought a lunatic home with him. He'd just saved her life, and somehow this girl seemed put out about it.

"I do," he said, falling into a seat by the dormant fireplace.

She studied the room with pursed lips, and some of his irritation with her behavior fled when he noticed how pale she looked.

"It's surprisingly...nice."

He let out a huff of amusement. "Take out the 'surprisingly' and your compliment might also have been nice."

To his delight, one corner of her mouth hitched up at that. "This is just not what I'd expect from..." She gestured toward him and it was impossible not to laugh.

"Oh no, do go on," he said, resting his arm on the settee's edge so he could slide down and make himself comfortable. "I would love to hear how that sentence will end."

She pursed her lips and looked away. Unwilling, it seemed, to outright insult him in his own home. Though he suspected he knew what she meant. She thought he was a pauper. Maybe even something worse. She had no idea who he really was, and for the moment, that was how he preferred it.

He had a feeling if she knew his father was a marquess, she'd behave entirely differently and that he could not bear. He liked this Delilah, the one that said whatever was on her mind, no matter how rude or thoughtless.

It was... Well, it was refreshing. She was cold lemonade on a hot day. Slightly sweet, a little sour, and anything but bland.

She turned to him suddenly, her arms wrapped around her waist as though she was cold—hard to imagine in this heat, but he supposed it could be shock.

The thought had him frowning, and his expression must have matched hers.

"You saved my life," she said suddenly.

His eyes widened in surprise at the shift in conversation. "You're welcome."

She stared at him for a long moment and he watched her swallow. "Thank you."

He nodded toward the end of the settee. "Have a seat."

She rubbed her arms. "No, thank you, I should—"

"Have a seat." His tone was less polite this time and he shifted forward, making more room for her as he eyed her steadily. "Please."

She blinked rapidly at the 'please' and he thought he saw confusion flicker in her eyes.

Poor thing had just been through the scare of her life and she was trying her best not to show it.

His heart did something strange. It made its presence known with a lurch. An inanimate monster coming to life, just like in that novel he'd recently read.

He shook off the thought with a rueful little laugh. It seemed they'd both been shaken by today's events.

She perched on the edge of the seat, her spine stiff and straight, her hands clasped daintily in her lap. When a servant entered and set the tray before her she blinked in surprise.

"I—I should not be here," she said slowly.

He knew what she meant. She should not be here alone with him. He knew it too. The problem was...he had no idea what else to do with her.

"I should go home," she said. Staring at the pot of tea before them but making no move to touch it.

"You should rest first." Even he was surprised by the softness of his voice. It felt like it had been an age since he'd talked to anyone like this—gently, as if to a child. He cleared his throat and moved forward, pouring the tea since she looked unfit to move. "You've been through an ordeal," he said. "You're shaken. Perhaps in shock—"

"I am no such thing," she said. "I am fine." As she said it she began to tremble and he muttered a curse under his breath.

In one move he was right next to her, his thigh pressed to hers as he wrapped an arm around her.

She stiffened even more. "What do you think you are—"

"Hush," he commanded. He held her tight, and after a heartbeat of holding herself stiffly, she collapsed against his side as though all the fight drained out of her at once.

She was warm and soft, and she smelled like heaven.

They sat like that for a long moment and he found himself wishing it wouldn't end.

It had to, of course. But he would have been content to sit like that for eternity.

"I should go home," she said when she finally stirred against his side. Her cheek rested against his heart and he wondered if she could feel the way it pounded heavily against his ribcage.

Of course, his heart had been working just fine his whole life, but he'd never been quite so aware of it before. He'd never *felt* it thudding away inside of him like this.

Like it wasn't his to control.

Like it no longer belonged to him.

Stuff and nonsense.

It wasn't until she made to move again that her words fully registered and when they did, it was with a thud.

She still didn't understand. Or maybe she just didn't wish to...

"You cannot go home, Delilah."

She pulled away from his arm and sat upright, adjusting her skirts as if that would lend this moment some decency. "Of course I can. I must. They will worry if—"

"Delilah." He leaned forward to see her face.

Her voice had an odd edge to it. She didn't *wish* to understand. But she was starting to. His heart did that lurch again, and he reached a hand out to cover hers, gentling his voice as he said her name again. "Delilah..."

"Don't." She pulled her hand from his. "Don't say it."

"You cannot go home, love—"

"Don't call me that."

He shifted to face her. "Delilah, listen to me."

She frowned, her lips pursing. She looked far more like herself, and he was glad, even as her pout made him sigh with frustration.

"It's Miss Clemmons," she snapped.

Stubborn little thing.

But that was how he liked her.

"Miss *Clemmons*..." He drew her name out exaggeratedly, making her scowl. "You cannot go home. You may not be safe there."

Her face drained of color. He hadn't thought she could grow any paler and he cursed himself for being responsible for her fear.

But what else could he do? She was in danger, and she had to know it.

"What happened just now," he said slowly, making sure she registered every word. "That was no accident."

Her lips parted on an intake of air and he reached for her. He didn't think about it; his body seemed to be acting on its own as he took her by the arms and drew her close.

Again, he wanted to kiss her. Kiss away her fear and replace the dazed look of shock with a dazed look of passion.

Instead he held her in his arms and showed restraint...to some extent.

She was in shock. Now was not the time for a flirtation, for heaven's sake.

"How can you be sure?" she asked, her voice breathless but strong.

She didn't try to pull out of the circle of his arms, and for that he was grateful. Whether she wanted to admit it or not, Delilah needed strength right now. She needed support. His arms braced her, held her upright, and though she fought it, he felt the moment she gave in a relaxed, letting him take some of her weight.

She nibbled on her lower lips, her gaze fixed on his chin, which likely needed a shave. Was it any wonder she thought him some uncouth vagabond? For the most part, he *was*. "If this wasn't an accident, it means...it would mean..." Her gaze lifted suddenly and met his.

He felt the directness of it like a punch in the gut.

"That would mean my fiancé meant to kill me."

He wanted to make her feel better, to cushion the blow. "Perhaps not kill..." he hedged.

Her eyes widened and he stopped speaking. He supposed offering the possibility of kidnapping would do little to ease her mind at this particular moment.

Her gaze was unbearably serious as it held his. "Are you certain it was not an accident, or..." She shrugged. "A coincidence, perhaps?"

He didn't answer, and it seemed he didn't have to.

She sighed and slumped against him. "I knew it."

He moved his head and accidentally nuzzled her hair. Well, perhaps it wasn't all that accidental. He shifted so they were once more comfortably seated, cuddled together in a way that would ruin them both were they to be discovered.

But this was his house, and his servants knew discretion.

And besides...she was a victim. He would help her, as he would any damsel in distress.

"Why do you say that?" he asked.

"Hmm?" She'd clearly gotten lost in her own thoughts as they sat.

"You said 'I knew it'," he reminded her.

"Oh, I... That is, I only meant, I..." She trailed off with a sigh. "I did something unforgivably stupid."

He stiffened. "What did you do?"

She leaned away from him just far enough to meet his gaze. "I tried to find proof."

His brows shot up. "You...you did *what*?"

She continued as if he hadn't interrupted. "And I was caught."

He let out a sharp exhale. "You *what*?"

She frowned. "Do you have a hearing problem, Mr. Calloway?"

To his surprise and hers a short laugh was shocked out of him. "I suppose the fact that your tongue hasn't lost its razor's edge means you are already on the road to recovery."

Her lips twitched for a second before she adopted an expression of ennui, as if she were bored by the evening's tedious adventure. "Now I suppose we need a plan."

"We?" he echoed.

"Of course *we*." She shot him a look. "Really, you must try to keep up, Mr. Calloway."

He laughed under his breath at her audacity. "I merely meant, don't you think you've done enough?"

She huffed in indignation as she crossed her arms, pulling back far enough that he was forced to drop his arms and release her. "If it weren't for me, you would have no proof that Everley is a criminal."

That had him straightening in surprise. "You have proof?"

She frowned and waved a hand in the direction of the door. "What do you call that back there in the carriage? That was proof, was it not? I shall tell the world that Everley tried to...to..." She blanched and stopped talking.

He sighed. "That is not *proof*, love. That's just your word against his."

"But you said—"

"I have no doubt it was not a coincidence," he said. "I saw a footman set off with a message just prior to your departure, and on top of that, the carriage took the wrong route."

She opened her mouth to speak but he spoke over her.

"But even so, that is not enough."

She shut her mouth with another huff.

"What exactly did he find you doing today? Take me through it step by step."

She talked rapidly, starting from the very beginning. She seemed to calm herself as she spoke. As if the very act of recounting it all helped her put it in perspective. For this reason, he found himself asking question after question, even when he'd gotten a good sense of all she had—and had not —discovered.

By the time they were done rehashing the day, the sun had fully set and the servants had brought them a cold supper of meats and bread before leaving them once more.

"So you found nothing in his desk," he said for the tenth time. Frustration had him tearing the bread in his hands with too much force. *Nothing.* He'd been so sure that Everley in all his arrogance would make a mistake. Leave evidence or at least some sort of clue that pointed to his next moves.

"Nothing," Delilah repeated with a sigh.

Delilah, for her part, was using a fork and knife and using dainty movements that seemed entirely out of place with the casual fare and atmosphere.

He suspected she was clinging to propriety for the normalcy it brought to this otherwise entirely abnormal day.

He dropped his food onto the plate and scrubbed a hand through his hair in frustration as he leaned back to study her. "What were he and your stepmother discussing?"

"Wedding plans, I presume."

"All day?" he asked. "Are weddings truly that complicated?"

She gave him a small smile and he felt his chest swell with pride. It was ridiculous the effect she had on him. It made no sense whatsoever, but now was not the time to try and sort it out.

"Weddings themselves might not be, but then there are the other matters," she said with a little wave of her fork.

"Other matters?"

"Yes. Dowries and such." She made a funny little face as she wrinkled her nose. "You know...the business of marriage."

He blinked at the note of bitterness in her voice and for the millionth time that day he felt a pang of sympathy for this odd girl with her snooty ways.

From a distance once might think she was just a spoiled wealthy young lady. But one would be wrong. She *was* that... but there was more to her than just that.

She just did a remarkable job of hiding it. But even so, her act didn't work on him.

He'd made a career out of learning people's real identities and ferreting out their true natures.

This girl wasn't nearly as shallow as she pretended, nor as

hardened. But he'd bet money he was one of few who knew that.

"You stepmother handles the...business of your marriage?" he asked.

She nodded. "It is not typical, I know, but my father is in ill health. He has been for years. My stepmother has all but taken over the day-to-day work with running an estate, and I am part of that estate."

She didn't sound sad and that casual mention of herself as just a part of her father's estate made him inexplicably angry.

"Most people would put their solicitor in charge, or appoint a guardian—"

She shook her head. "My father doesn't trust many people, and he trusts no one as much as he does his wife."

He eyed her. "Are you and your father close?"

The flinch was so subtle one might have missed it. Rupert did not.

"No."

No. That was it. No explanations or justifications. Just no.

"It is getting late," she said, setting down her utensils as she looked toward the dark window. "I had better get home."

He gaped at her. She couldn't be serious. "You are not going home. You would not be safe there."

She huffed. "Fine. Then I will go back to the school. I'm certain Miss Grayson will have my room—"

"You cannot go there, either."

She blinked. "Why not?"

He glowered at her as he leaned forward. "Do you honestly think Miss Grayson or any of the other girls could keep you safe if trouble follows?"

She opened her mouth but he wasn't done.

"Would you want to be responsible for putting them in harm's way?"

She blinked and clamped her mouth shut. "Then..." Her cheeks stained pink. "W-where shall I go?"

His heart threatened to combust with emotions at the rare display of vulnerability. "You're not going anywhere, love." He reached for her hand. "I'm afraid you'll have to stay here."

8

She stared at this strange man in horror. "*Here?*" Her voice rose an octave higher than usual without her say so. "You want me to stay *here?*"

He shrugged, as if he hadn't just suggested that they ruin her reputation in one rash move.

"That is ridiculous."

He leaned back, looking far too amused for her liking. She hated when this man laughed at her, and it seemed to be most of the time.

The rest of the time he was being even more irritating by comforting her like she was a child or someone to be pitied.

She was neither. She was Miss Delilah Clemmons and while her situation might not have been ideal, it was not dire.

She hadn't died today, after all.

That was a good start.

And that was very much thanks to this man.

She shoved the thought to the side. She was grateful for his assistance, yes, but she couldn't afford to focus on that now or she might forget that he was not her friend.

He was a stranger.

A stranger who'd held her in his arms and made her feel safe, a stranger and who'd appeared out of nowhere when she'd needed him, a stranger who'd saved her life...

But still a stranger.

She looked around her at the uncommonly nice surroundings and she was reminded once again of just how little she knew about him.

What kind of man looked like he did—the very picture of gruff and disheveled—but lived in a place like this?

"Do you live alone?" she asked.

He nodded slowly. "Just me and a few servants."

"And you expect me to stay here. Overnight."

"I do."

She let out a shaky breath. "I cannot do that."

He met her stare for a long moment, and she hated him for it. Those rough features that looked as though he'd been in too many fights. The broad, muscular shoulders that didn't seem to fit in this elegant home. His frame was too big for the furniture, it seemed...

But the perfect fit for her to lean against.

She shut her eyes to stop herself from going there. It was bad enough that she'd let him hold her—twice.

It was even worse that she'd enjoyed it.

But now they were discussing her ruin, thank you very much. This was definitely *not* the time to swoon. "I cannot," she said again.

"Why not?"

Her eyes grew so wide, it actually started to hurt. But honestly... "Are you serious?"

He shrugged, like they were discussing the weather. "Of course. You cannot go home, you shouldn't go to the school... where do you think you ought to go?"

Her mind raced to think of other options. She had no

family to speak of aside from her father, no friends other than the girls at the school...

She was alone.

The weight of this realization hit her so hard and so quick, she didn't have time to brace for it. Once when she was a child, she fell from a low tree branch and the air from her lungs had left in a rush. She couldn't draw in a breath right away and there had been this moment of panic as she fought for air.

That was exactly how she felt now. Like she could not breathe. Like she might *never* be able to breathe.

"Easy, love." He moved to her, drew her out of her seat and held her like a child, cradling her to his chest and stroking her back, her hair. "I've got you," he murmured. "I have you."

She clutched the fabric of his shirt. Her heart was racing too fast, her hands shaking, and her eyes...

Oh drat. She squeezed them shut, willing away the tears.

It was the shock of it all, that was all.

His hands on her back were so large and so warm. So rough she could feel his callouses through the thin material of her dress.

When her breathing started to slow, he pulled back to look down at her and the threat of tears started all over again at the tenderness she saw there. His dark eyes were filled with a warmth she'd never seen before.

A warmth that wasn't friendship and wasn't familial—and yet it made her feel loved.

Ridiculous, obviously. But it helped to soothe her all the same.

"I'll have Mrs. Tate ready a room for you," he said.

She gulped, wanting to protest but knowing she'd lost this argument.

She bit her lip as she tried to resign herself to this new reality. "My family will be worried when I do not return."

He eyed her steadily and she wondered if he knew that she was lying. There was every chance no one would even notice.

"We can send word that you are well."

She frowned. "You wish me to tell them that I am *well*. That I am merely staying at a strange man's home. Nothing to worry about."

His lips twitched at her sarcasm. "I'd thought perhaps we could lie. Tell them you decided to stay at the school for the night."

She nodded slowly. "I could say that I went there to see friends and lost track of time, perhaps." Her voice trailed off. The details of her lie didn't really matter. Her stepmother would likely be pleased to have her out of the house for a while and her father...

Well, she wasn't even sure he knew she'd been staying with them.

She sighed. "Very well. I suppose I will have to talk to Miss Grayson tomorrow. Let her know what is happening so she can lie on my behalf should anyone ask."

He nodded. "I'll go with you."

She wanted to argue but the truth was, she wasn't certain she'd feel safe without him at her side.

"Come," he said. "Let us get you situated so you can rest."

She nodded, letting him lead her toward the door. She stopped as the biggest fear of all had her worrying her lower lip. "What will we say if anyone discovers that I've been staying here...with you?"

He eyed her for a long moment, and when he spoke his voice was low and even. "If that happens, we will just have to wed."

9

The moment the words came out of his mouth, he knew it was a mistake.

Or rather, he knew that it was a mistake to say it *aloud*.

He also realized at the same exact time, that it was a mistake to say it aloud because…he meant it. He *would* marry her if it meant keeping her and her reputation safe. He stared at her blankly as the realization hit home.

He wasn't certain who was more horrified.

She broke the silence with a wail. "I cannot marry *you*."

Well then. It seemed Delilah was definitely the more horrified of the two.

"Then let us hope it does not come to that," he said, hoping the end the discussion.

But she continued to gape at him in horror. "I *cannot* marry you," she said again, changing the emphasis as though he might not have understood.

"Yes, you have said that already." He kept his voice low and even. This conversation had to end. Now. He wasn't an overly proud man. He'd never deluded himself into thinking he was so devastatingly handsome to those of the fairer sex. He knew he had none of the charm and manners that a young woman like Delilah expected. He'd been out of society too long to remember all that was proper and pleasing to a lady. And yet...

"I cannot *marry* you." She was shaking her head now and looked frighteningly close to tears at the thought.

"Yes," he said. "You have made this very clear."

His pride stung. He could admit it. He'd never actually proposed to a lady before—in fact, up until tonight, he'd assumed he'd continue his life as a bachelor quite contentedly. From the moment he'd opted to live outside society and pursue justice instead of the life of a gentleman, he'd understood that he was likely not fit to marry. At least not a lady of the *ton*.

It was a lonely life he'd chosen, and he had no qualms with that. There were moments, of course, on long and lonely assignments, when perhaps he'd considered what it would be to have a partner to come home to, but even in those fantasies he'd known better than to imagine some society darling. No, what he needed was a helpmate. A woman with skills and prowess of her own. Someone strong who could face the dangers that came with his line of work.

Someone he wouldn't have to worry about.

"I just...I meant to say..." She shook her head, apparently now too horrified to piece words together. Which was for the best as he had an inkling what she was about to say.

Again.

Sure enough... "I cannot—"

"Marry me. Yes, I understand that very well, Miss Clemmons. Your point has been made." *But you might not have a choice.*

He did not say that, of course.

The poor girl was only just now recovering from her

earlier shock. Her life had gone through an epic upheaval, and he couldn't expect her to now understand and comprehend the fact that her life plans, such as they were, may have been forever altered.

"But I might have to," she said, a high, breathless note in her voice hinting at hysteria. "That's what you mean to say. I might have to marry you or risk total ruin."

He studied her with increasing alarm.

She'd clearly been in shock earlier, just after the accident. That had been expected. Her life had been in danger, and her world turned upside down.

But he suspected she was only now beginning to see the ramifications. She was just now beginning to understand that the life she'd been meant to live might never come about.

She might just end up a scandal. Or worse, stuck with a man like him.

"I-I...Y-You—" Her voice was edging up, and her breathing was coming in dangerously shallow gasps. Her eyes were unfocused and her hands fluttered helplessly at her side.

And all at the thought of marrying me.

He tried not to take it personally, he truly did. "Hush, Delilah," he said, taking a small step forward, afraid of alarming her further, but wanting to comfort her all the same.

For a man who'd eschewed polite society to build a life of independence, competence, and strength, it was a rare moment indeed to find himself so incredibly...useless.

When she didn't try to back away he took another step forward. Her eyes were darting about and her breathing was growing so erratic, he feared she might faint. "There, there." He reached out to pat her arm. It was meant to be consoling but just seemed rather awkward.

He wasn't sure what his problem was. Twice this afternoon he'd held her in his arms, more intimately than he'd ever held anyone, truth be told.

But that was before he'd gone and mentioned marriage. And now...

Well, now it was impossible not to look at her and imagine what it might be like if he could hold her like that at any time. Not because she feared for her safety, not for any particular reason at all. But just because she was his to hold. To protect and to cherish.

The air rushed from his lungs as a wave of emotion hit him like a tidal wave.

Never before had he even contemplated marriage, and now it was all he could imagine.

More alarmingly, it was all he *wanted*.

But not just any marriage...

Her wild gaze finally met his and his heart stalled in his chest as something seemed to pass between them, a physical but invisible connection that had his heart stuttering back into action with a painful thud against his ribcage.

He wanted to marry *her*.

To his surprise, she took a step toward him, her hands reaching out until they were pressed to his chest. "What am I going to do, Mr. Calloway? My life is over."

He wasn't sure what affected him more. The pitiable words or the feel of her touch as her fingers pressed into him, clutching the fabric of his jacket like a lifeline.

She needed him. Maybe not forever, maybe not even after tomorrow, but for now, she needed him to be strong for her.

And with that thought, his wounded pride was forgotten, and his selfish wishes pushed to the side.

He wrapped his arms around her and pulled her in closer. "We will figure this out," he said softly. His voice was firm. It was a promise. A vow. And one he meant to keep. "I will never let Everley harm you."

"But he's to be my husband," she said, her voice little more than a whisper. "My father promised me to him. And you said it yourself. It is my suspicions against a gentleman's word. No one will believe me."

He watched her throat work as she swallowed. "My own father might not believe me." She shut her eyes as she clearly struggled for control. "He might not care."

He had no idea what to say to that but his heart broke at the pain that flickered across those beautiful, delicate features. He doubted anyone had ever seen this strong, proud woman so vulnerable, and the thought that she was opening up to him, of all people, was humbling, even as he told himself that it was only because he was here.

He was her only option.

Her eyes fluttered open and once more he forgot all about reason and all about pride. "What if he comes after me again? What if my father insists on the wedding?" Her voice was growing hysterical again and tears now welled in her eyes.

Everything in him ached with the need to help her. To calm her. To...distract her, at the very least.

"What if no one believes me? What if—"

He kissed her.

They both froze as his lips crushed hers. What was he doing? He didn't know. And at this particular moment, he didn't care. The scent of her, the feel of her in his arms, the taste of her soft lips...

All combined, it washed away every intelligent thought in a heartbeat.

Her lips parted slightly on a gasp and he moved against her, tasting her sweetness, teasing her until she kissed him back. Lightly at first. Tentatively. Her hands still pressed to his chest, she came to life in his arms, slowly and exquisitely.

He forced himself to move slowly, keeping his hands on her back as he explored the softness of her lips, as he reveled in the sweet intimacy of her breath mingling with his.

Her fingers curled into his flesh as she leaned forward,

deepening the kiss as their lips clung together, no longer teasing but tasting. Exploring.

The summer heat had nothing on the flow of lava in his veins that made him feel possessed with the need to hold her closer, to kiss her deeper, to clutch her to his heart and never let go.

The sound of a servant in the hallway, heading toward the stairs to ready a room for his guest broke through his haze and had him pulling back reluctantly.

Her breathing was still uneven, but she no longer looked like she might faint. Her eyes were still closed, her lips still parted—

Perfection. She was utter perfection.

When she opened her eyes, he saw her surprise. No doubt it matched his. It wasn't as though he'd *planned* to kiss her.

She blinked once. Twice. Then she took a step back and he dropped his arms to let her go.

"What was—"

"Go get some rest, Delilah." He cut off her questions... questions he wasn't quite sure how to answer. "Mrs. Tate will show you to your room and make sure you are comfortable."

She shut her mouth and nodded, shuffling backwards toward the door.

"Everything will be clearer in the morning," he promised.

10

The next morning *nothing* was clearer.

Delilah nibbled on a pastry Mrs. Tate had brought her along with tea and a basin of water to freshen herself.

If anything, she was more confused than ever.

She had half a mind to tell Mr. Calloway that he was a liar. Making promises he couldn't keep.

Like promising to *marry* her.

Her mouth stopped working mid-chew. Her heart did that thing it had taken to doing lately. It seemed to be attempting an escape, and every time it happened, it stole her breath and made her insides ache.

He'd offered to marry her. The crazy man with the nice home and lovely servants had offered to marry her.

She looked around her. How did he afford all this as a private investigator? She supposed it would be rude to ask.

Although, rudeness rarely stopped her from anything. It certainly hadn't stopped her from refusing his marriage offer.

She winced and shoved the rest of the pastry into her

mouth all at once, as if a mound of sugar might tamper the guilt and humiliation.

She might not be known for her sweet nature, but even she knew better than to insult the man who'd saved her life.

She hadn't meant to, but the unexpected proposal had been the proverbial last straw.

For the first time since her carriage had come under attack, she'd honestly feared for her life. Not because she thought Mr. Calloway would hurt her. Her heart did that silly move again as she remembered the way he'd treated her yesterday. He'd been nothing but kind and caring. For a man who looked so brutish, he'd been surprisingly gentle with her.

On top of that, he'd done the unthinkable and made her feel safe and secure.

Until he'd mentioned marriage. Up until that moment she hadn't really given much thought about the future. She hadn't been able to as she'd been consumed with fears for her imminent safety.

But with that odd half-proposal, she'd realized with a start—her life might never be the same. It had shaken her to her core and she'd spoken without thought, fear and confusion winning out over any sort of politeness or etiquette.

She sighed as she swallowed the last of the pastry. Sugar did indeed help her nerves. As did the morning light streaming through the window. It was hard to feel terrified of an ominous fiancé when she was safe and well-fed with the sun shining and birds chirping outside her window.

And yet...what she would do next?

That was still unclear.

How Mr. Calloway would ensure Lord Everley did not hurt her again?

Equally unclear.

And then there was the matter of her father. She would have to explain to her father that she could not perform the one duty she'd been raised to perform. Her sole reason for existing in this family was to make a good match, and now...

Now she had no idea where she'd end up or with whom.

The only thing clear was just how uncertain her future was.

She did her best to freshen her appearance but was forced to wear the same gown as the day before. She pinched her cheeks to try and ward off the pallor that was making her look like a ghost.

Fear for one's life tended to wreak havoc on one's complexion, she now knew. This was a life lesson she could have done without.

When at last she could not delay the inevitable, she found herself walking slowly down the steps toward the dining room, where she'd been told she could find the master of the house.

A whole new set of nerves had her steeling her spine and tilting up her chin. These nerves had nothing to do with her safety and everything to do with seeing the man who had kissed her last night.

Her first kiss...and oh, what a kiss.

She stopped in the hallway just outside the dining room, giving herself a moment to let her silly heart do that ridiculous dance and waiting for her insides to settle.

It was just a kiss.

A big deal to her, of course, but it had likely meant nothing to him. The best thing to do was to ignore it. Pretend it never happened. Emotions had been high and the situation tense.

Kisses were likely to sprout up at times like that. Like smelling salts. Or a cup of tea.

Kisses were just a way of calming one's nerves. Everyone knew that.

She clasped her hands together, single-mindedly ignoring

the voice of reason that told her last night's kiss had done nothing to calm her. It had done the opposite, in fact.

She'd lain awake for hours replaying that kiss as her heart had thudded in her chest like a runaway horse.

And now she was frozen, stuck standing in a hallway because her silly heart was overreacting. Her belly too. Her entire body seemed to be suffering a fit of nerves, and over what...?

A meaningless kiss.

"He's just in there, miss," a servant kindly pointed out, as though she were lost.

Delilah nodded her thanks. There was nothing for it but to face him. Head held high, a smile on her face, and her heart firmly in its proper place.

"Good morning," she said as she entered.

Mr. Calloway was finished with his meal, it seemed, and was stretched back in his seat with a newspaper spread wide before him. "Morning," he muttered, never looking up as he scowled down at the news.

"Not a morning person, are we?" she asked lightly.

He grunted.

She grinned. Her tension dissolved a bit at the normalcy of it all. Well, not *normal*. She couldn't say she'd ever had breakfast alone with a gentleman she barely knew before.

Though she wasn't sure she could continue thinking of him as a stranger, she realized as she sank into the seat opposite him.

She studied him now, from his too-long, far too disheveled hair, to the blunt nose, the seemingly permanent stubble on his chin... She had a visceral memory of how that stubble had felt when he'd kissed her. The surprisingly delicious feel of his rough skin against her sensitive flesh.

She shivered.

No, he was definitely not a stranger anymore. Which begged the question...what was he?

Friend? Ally?

"Would you like something to eat?" he asked abruptly, finally looking up to consider her. "Mrs. Tate can prepare something for you. I don't normally eat breakfast but I'm sure she'd be willing to—"

"I already ate, thank you," she said. She found herself battling a grin.

Ridiculous, really. She had far too many concerns in front of her to be smiling like a dolt over this man's brash morning behavior.

It was rather endearing to see him ill at ease, though. Their every other encounter had left her feeling as though she were an overly sensitive shrill beast in the face of his calm, laid-back demeanor.

This morning he looked far more like a bear than a man.

"What are you smiling about?" he asked warily.

She gave her head a shake and wiped any trace of a smile from her lips. "I just didn't know you were so disgruntled in the mornings, that is all."

He grunted again and ran a hand through his hair, mussing it even further. "Yes, well. I didn't get much sleep last night." His glower seemed to indicate that this was her fault, and the urge to smile died as surely as her smile.

Oh.

She shifted uncomfortably under his glare.

He'd been up thinking about her plight, no doubt. Perhaps wondering just how he'd gotten stuck with an ungrateful brat when he'd only been hired to investigate Everley.

Or maybe he'd been regretting that kiss.

The thought stung.

Or wishing he could take back his proposal.

That cut like a knife.

She fiddled with a ribbon on her gown and avoided looking directly at his furrowed expression. Of those options, she supposed she preferred the first so she chose to address that. "I will compensate you for your efforts, of course."

He stilled in the act of reaching for his tea. "Pardon me?"

She licked her lips only to find that her entire mouth was as dry as the desert. "Perhaps I will have another cup of tea, after all," she said, craning her neck as if she might find Mrs. Tate hiding behind the cupboard.

"You will *pay* me," he said slowly, his tone incredulous.

"Er, yes," she said, her voice pitching up at the end as though it were a question. She huffed in exasperation with herself. What was it about this man that brought out the worst in her?

Where were her cool, pleasing manners that she wielded so handily around gentlemen of the *ton*? She'd spent a lifetime perfecting the art of prudent flirtation and tinkling laughter, only to have it fail her whenever this brute was in her presence.

She cleared her throat, and tried again, with a small smile this time. "What I meant to say is...I realize that you were hired by Tolston for one particular job, and now you have been saddled with me." She paused, humiliation threatening to stop her words altogether. "You went above and beyond the call of duty yesterday, and I would like to ensure that you receive proper compensation."

His glower never wavered and then after a heartbeat of studying her a flicker of amusement broke through that dour expression and he burst out in a laugh that had her cheeks bursting into flame.

She kept her composure, however, as she clasped her hands in her lap. "I did not think I said anything so amusing."

He gave his head a little shake. "You will *pay* me," he

muttered again under his breath, like he still could not believe it.

She opened her mouth to ask him just why he was laughing at her, but then she saw it.

A flicker of hurt beneath the mirth.

Oh drat. The words died on her tongue. She'd hurt his feelings.

She bit her lip. She should be used to this feeling. Her tongue had a tendency to sting, even when she wasn't trying to be mean. That was why Prudence had been her only friend for a while there, until Louisa and Addie had decided to overlook her flaws.

Prudence never took her seriously. The others were learning not to.

But this man...a man who looked so strong and...well, untouchable really. She couldn't have hurt this man.

Could she?

She scrambled to think of a good apology, but apologizing had never been her strong suit. "I only meant—"

"With what?" he interrupted.

She blinked. "Pardon me?"

He leaned forward slowly and she was reminded of a large cat, hunting its prey. "With what do you mean to pay me for saving your life and keeping you safe?"

"Uh..." She swallowed at the predatory look in his eyes. Not cruel, like Everley, just...disconcerting. She wasn't sure anyone had ever looked at her with such intensity before, and certainly not a man.

Definitely not a man she'd kissed.

And there she went, thinking about that kiss again. Her cheeks must have been scarlet if the heat scorching her cheeks was any indication.

"You are right, of course," she said with as much humility as she could muster.

It wasn't much.

She looked down at her lap as his meaning hit home. She came from wealth. She'd been spoiled with every gift she'd ever asked for. She only had to tell her nurse or governess what she desired, and it appeared as if by magic.

But money...*actual* money...

Her only wealth was in the form of a dowry. "I, uh...I..." She swallowed. "I could marry you."

His eyes flared wide, the amusement gone in a flash. She couldn't tell what he was thinking, but she knew what *she* was thinking and it made her want to cry.

Was that why he'd offered to marry her the night before? Did he think he'd won himself a golden goose when he'd saved her life and potentially ruined her reputation?

Even as she thought it, she kicked herself for thinking it. The man had been nothing but kind to her, she ought not be suspecting him of mercenary motives.

Her gaze collided with his and she could not read him at all. He was staring at her with the same amount of intensity, but she could not read his thoughts.

She forced the hurt feelings down. Deep, deep down to some hidden place where she might eventually pull them out and analyze them. But for now, this was a stranger who'd done right by her.

Whether his offer to marry her had been fueled by a desire for her fortune or not, it did not matter.

Besides, he had every right to wish for some sort of payment for the noble act he'd undertaken.

It showed he was sensible, really.

She tilted her chin up higher. "I do not know that my father would honor the dowry he's promised to Everley. But I know he would ensure that I was well settled. And once he learned of the circumstances leading to the...the..."

He arched his brows. "The marriage?" he offered.

She nodded. "Once he understood that you'd saved my life, I am certain he would...provide handsomely."

She thought. She hoped. She bit her lip. Oh drat, what if he *didn't*?

Her father was not a warm man, and they had never been close. He took pride in having a beautiful, marriageable daughter who could ensure a good match.

But if she couldn't?

What value did she have?

She looked down at the table as the truth hit home.

She had none.

Not to her family, at least.

Perhaps Mr. Calloway sensed the change in her, because he sighed from across the table. "Let us shelve all talk of compensation and marriage for the time being, shall we?" His voice sounded weary. "For now let us just focus on the task at hand, which is to keep you safe from harm."

She nodded, her throat still too choked to speak.

"Come," he said, his voice sounded far more normal—all gruff and low and at ease as he came to stand. "We shall visit your School of Charm and ensure that they understand your predicament. I've already told Tolston to meet us there."

She felt a smile tugging at her lips as she lifted her gaze. "It could not have been difficult to convince him. Lord Tolston will find any excuse to spend time with his future wife."

He smiled in return and she felt warm all the way through at the affection in his eyes.

The awkwardness from a moment ago was gone, and they were back to being...

Friends.

Allies?

Oh, whatever they were, they were back.

11

Rupert tried not to notice the whispering that was taking place the other side of the door.

Miss Grayson smiled kindly. "Do not mind the girls, they are just curious." She glanced over at Delilah. "And worried."

Delilah looked away.

"Tolston and I will only tell them as much as you wish to let them know," Miss Grayson said to Delilah.

Delilah sniffed, her haughty expression speaking volumes —to Rupert, at least. She was uncomfortable with Miss Grayson's kindness, unused to being the object of concern.

"Whatever you please," Delilah said stiffly. "I leave it to your discretion."

Tolston, who'd arrived at the same time they had, looked to Delilah as well. "We will get to the bottom of this, Miss Clemmons."

She nodded, but her confidence was feigned. He could not blame her. Rupert had been trying to affix a crime to Everley's name for years and had never made progress. What were the odds that they could do so now, with her wedding date looming in the not-too-distant future?

Miss Grayson reached a hand out to Delilah but seemed to think better of it and snatched it back. "Should we not tell your father? Your stepmother?"

Did Delilah have any idea how much her silence gave away? How her eyes spoke volumes even when she kept her mouth shut.

She did not believe they would care, or maybe she just was not certain they would believe her. Either way, every time her family had been mentioned, she'd drawn into herself in a way that made Rupert want to rage.

He could handle her anger, he now knew how to soothe her when she was frightened, but this... Her withdrawing into herself, not trusting the people around her with her emotions—it drove him mad.

Specifically, it made him want to rail against the person or people who had instilled this level of distrust. Who had raised her to be a veritable hermit crab. All hard shell on the outside, and a soft underbelly she was terrified to expose.

Miss Grayson and Tolston were waiting patiently for her to answer the direct question about her family, perhaps not realizing what a sensitive topic they'd touched upon.

When he could stand it no longer, Rupert answered on her behalf. "I've advised Miss Clemmons to keep this business as confidential as possible for the time being. As her father is sick and ought not to suffer undue stress. I believe it would be for the best if we wait to speak to him until we have conclusive proof."

He looked over and found Delilah staring at him, her expression inscrutable.

He turned back to the others. "We're only sharing this information with you because we may need your help to keep Delilah's reputation intact," he said.

Miss Grayson nodded. "Of course. We will do whatever you need."

Delilah stepped in with the details of the message she wished for Miss Grayson to send to her home. That she had decided to stay at the school for a while to see her friends.

"Of course I will send that," she said, concern tightening Miss Grayson's pretty features. "But...to stay at the home of a bachelor, unchaperoned..."

"It is not ideal," Delilah said, her tone dry. "But it is where I am safe."

Rupert wasn't certain, but he suspected his chest puffed to double its size at that show of confidence that he could keep her safe.

He *would*.

He had no doubt of that. He'd give his life before he let any harm come to her.

But the fact that she knew it too—that was a boon to his pride.

Once Miss Grayson was appeased and had gone off to her writing desk in the corner to compose the missive, Tolston turned the conversation back to more pressing business.

"So, after all that...are we really no closer to having any proof that Everley is the man behind so many crimes?"

Rupert sighed. "I'm afraid so."

Tolston gave Delilah a sidelong look that Rupert could well interpret. *Time is running out.*

"We have plenty of circumstantial evidence," Tolston said. "Perhaps with our testimony... I mean, having the Earl of Tolston and Lord—" He stopped himself when Rupert's eyes narrowed. "Er, a distinguished fellow like yourself, Calloway." Sitting back in his seat, Tolston crossed his arms over his chest. "Would that not be enough?"

"I'm afraid not," he muttered. Rupert was still shifting uncomfortably at the use of the title. It had been an age since he'd gone by the honorary title, and it didn't sit right. It never had. Unlike his father and elder brother, he'd never seemed meant for the peerage. He was too big, too unrefined, too uninterested in societal politics, and even less interested in learning how to charm and persuade.

He glanced over at Delilah to see if she had heard but she seemed to be lost in her own thoughts.

What would she think if she knew he was the second son of a marquess?

He felt his lips quirk with rueful humor. Would she still offer to pay him? He'd admit, that had stung.

Worse, would she offer to marry him like she was some commodity he might accept in lieu of coins?

He gave his head a little shake. Delilah's safety was what was at stake and he had to focus.

Tolston heaved a weary sigh that echoed his sentiments exactly. "So then, what do we do next?"

He'd been pondering that all night—well, when he wasn't reliving that kiss. He'd tossed and turned the night before, torn between concern for her safety and the desire to wake her just so he could relive that kiss.

"Unfortunately our best lead is at the docks, but we don't have any specifics." Rupert shook his head in irritation. "I still think our clues lie in his home somewhere—we know he conducts his business there. I had my chance to search and I failed." He glanced over at Delilah. Not that he could call their first interaction a *failure*.

It had been monumental. Life changing...

But no help in the course of his investigation.

"If we knew he'd be out of the house, I could attempt to break into his office again, I suppose," he said, rubbing the back of his neck as he thought. "But we'd need to know ahead of time that he'd be gone."

He was about to suggest they send someone to bribe a servant when Delilah chimed in.

"Tomorrow evening."

Both men turned to look at her.

"Pardon?" Tolston said.

She licked her lips. "He has an appointment tomorrow evening with someone named Albert on Rivington Street. I saw it in his diary."

The gentlemen continued to stare at her in silence. Rupert's brain clicked into gear for what felt like the first time since that kiss had addled him. Albert. Rivington. "What time?"

Her gaze shifted upward as she searched her memory. "Nine o'clock."

He and Tolston exchanged a look.

"Why? What is it?" Delilah asked.

He couldn't help it. He laughed. Tolston grinned as well. Rupert did not wish to put the cart before the horse, but his gut told him this was it.

This was precisely the bit of information he'd been trying to find.

"Why are you laughing?" Delilah demanded, her tone delightfully peevish. He turned to find her scowling at him and he laughed harder.

Oh yes, he much preferred this Delilah. She was much more fun to tease.

"I'm laughing at you, silly girl."

Her frown deepened and he leaned toward her with a grin. "You are absolutely brilliant, did you know that?"

Her eyes widened in surprise, a smile tugging at her lips as she gave him a look of wary amusement. "Of course I know that," she shot back. She folded her hands primly. "But why exactly do *you* know that?"

He and Tolston filled her in on the fact that Albert was

the name of a dock and Rivington was street near the wharf that was lined with warehouses for storage.

"You just asked if there was anything suspicious in his diary," she muttered defensively. "How was I supposed to know any of this?"

"You weren't," he assured her. "But now that we know..."

"We can finally end this," Tolston finished.

The very thought of finally bringing justice to the man who murdered his best friend just to inherit the title...it should have brought a world of relief. His best friend's so-call *accident* and Rupert's suspicions around it were why he'd chosen this life in the first place.

It had all begun with Everley, and Rupert's inability to prove him responsible for murder.

And now it was within his grasp and...

He was worried.

Blast it all. He was too worried to truly enjoy this new turn. His mind was already on Delilah, and what this would mean for her future.

12

Delilah listened as the two men sketched out a plan for the following night.

She was to stay here at the school as they and their men descended on Everley, hoping to catch him in the midst of a dastardly act.

Mr. Calloway had assured her no less than ten times now that he'd have ample security posted at and around the school's premises.

"We will ensure that all of you are safe," Tolston added.

She had no doubt that Tolston would move heaven and hell to make sure that Addie was protected. Her gaze met Mr. Calloway's and her breath caught in her throat when she realized...

He would do the same for her.

Annoying, uncalled for tears stung the back of her eyes.

Mercy, what was happening to her? She was never this emotional about *anything*.

She supposed nearly dying was a valid excuse.

She dropped her gaze, unable to hold it any longer because... He would see.

That was the thing about Mr. Calloway. He seemed to see everything. Too much. The way he'd been looking at her earlier, she'd wanted to get up out of her seat and run.

Instead, she'd born Miss Grayson's kindness and Tolston's concern and Mr. Calloway's...

Well, she wasn't sure what exactly he'd been feeling. She had no earthly idea what he even thought of her. But he *was* protective of her and seemed to genuinely care about her survival.

Maybe even her happiness.

I'll marry you.

She gave her head a shake as she chided herself for even thinking it. He was a gentleman, that was all. He might not have a title or be a powerful man of society, but he'd clearly been raised to be a gentleman.

She frowned down at her lap. Not for the first time she found herself curious about his upbringing. He had the manners of a knight, the appearance of a street thug, and the attitude of...she knew not what.

He was at once arrogant, competent, caring, and unconcerned with society. He was an oddity, to be sure.

But where had he come from?

Perhaps he was a bastard—raised in a lord's house, but not a true gentleman.

She risked a peek in his direction. Yes, that would perhaps explain his odd conflicting behaviors.

When at last it was time to leave, a plan was in place, and she was exhausted. Perhaps she ought to be anxious or fearful of what was to come, but as she said her goodbyes to Miss Grayson and the others, all she felt was weary exhaustion.

The entire carriage ride back she found herself sorting through all that had happened. Her mind racing to connect the dots and find a pattern in the chaos that was now her life.

There was something missing. A piece to the puzzle she could not quite place...

"Are you all right?" Mr. Calloway's low voice, filled with concern, had her looking over quickly.

"Fine," she said automatically. "I am fine."

He studied her profile. "You do not have to be, you know."

The carriage drew to a halt and she was saved from having to respond. He got out first and held out a hand.

As she took it and let him lead her into his home, she found herself wondering at the normalcy of this. At what point had she become complacent about traveling alone with an unwed man, or at entering his home and feeling like...

Feeling like it was *her* home, too.

She stopped in the entryway. She'd stayed here all of one night and yet she felt more comfortable here with him than she had staying at her own childhood home.

What did that say about her? About her life? About where she belonged?

"You look as though you could use a glass of sherry." His voice was laced with amusement but concern etched his brow, making his gruff appearance that much more intimidating. "Come."

He led her into the parlor. The same warm, cozy room where he'd brought her the day before.

She liked it in here. In this dark, wood-paneled room she felt as though the rest of the world might not exist. Like she was taking a seat in a place out of time, where it was just her and Mr. Calloway.

For the remainder of today, at least, it *was* just the two of them. And that was an utter relief.

He waited until she took a sip of sherry and winced. She never *had* liked the drink.

"Feeling better?" he asked.

She nodded, lying out of habit, before remembering who she was talking to. "Not really."

Her honesty was rewarded by a small smile of understanding. "You have been through much these past two days."

She nibbled on her lip and toyed with the glass as she considered that. "To be honest, I have not been entirely at ease since I learned of my engagement. But yes, over these past two days…the situation has certainly grown more dire."

He studied her as he leaned back on the settee beside her. They'd taken their positions from the evening before as if it was a habit. A routine. Like they were an old married couple who had their usual spots beside one another.

Old married couple? What a silly idea. She set the sherry down. That was likely responsible for her ridiculous notions.

"So, you were not set on marrying him then?"

Her head came up suddenly. "Of course not."

He arched a brow. "You seemed awfully intent on it at your engagement ball the other night."

Shame shot through her at the way she'd defended the man even though she hadn't known him. "Yes, well…" She trailed off with a shrug. "I suppose I didn't want to believe that my father would hand me over to a ne'er-do-well, least of all a criminal."

His silence had her shifting uncomfortably. She wasn't sure what she'd been looking for by admitting to that, but now that it was in the open, she regretted it.

And yet, now that it was in the open, she could not let it go.

"Do you think he knew?" She forced herself to look over at him, dreading the pity she would find there.

But there was no pity, only sympathy. Affection, even.

She tore her gaze away.

Dratted sherry. It made her see things that could not be

there. She'd been nothing but horrible to this man. She was his obligation, that was all. His burden, at best.

She licked her lips as she stared straight ahead and rephrased the question that he clearly did not wish to answer. "Do you think my father knew that Everley is...who he is."

Cruel. Criminal. Evil.

"I do not know," Mr. Calloway said slowly, warily. "Your father has been out of society for some time now, has he not? I suppose it is possible that he was ignorant of Lord Everley's true nature."

Possible, but not probable. She knew that was what he meant. His attempt to spare her feelings by offering up that optimistic suggestion made the truth that much harder to bear. "I wish I could believe that."

It came out on a whisper and to her despair, tears welled in her eyes before she quickly blinked them away.

His hand covered hers on the seat between them. She was glad that he didn't try to comfort her, to tell her that she was wrong and that her father only had her best interests at heart.

She wouldn't have believed him anyway and lying would not have suited him. "My father might not be an active participant in society since his health has taken a turn, but he has eyes and ears everywhere. And he's done business with Everley for a long time."

Mr. Calloway stayed silent as she tried to reconcile herself to the fact that her father hadn't cared one whit about her happiness. She'd never dreamt that he would put her wishes first when it came to finding a match, but she'd never thought he would knowingly choose someone who might hurt her.

The thought left her cold. So cold she reached for the sherry again.

"I was such a fool," she said softly. "For wanting to trust my father. For blindly placing my faith in Everley..." She shook her head in shame at the way she'd stood up for him to this man that night in Everley's study.

"You could not have known," he said.

"*You* knew," she said, accusation in her voice, though what she was accusing him of she wasn't certain. Perhaps she was just accusing herself of being a dolt and she'd turned that tone on the wrong person.

She was the one at fault here, not he.

He shifted to face her better. "I only knew because Everley and I have a history."

She stilled. All day today she'd told herself that she barely knew this man. One kiss and a magnificent rescue did not mean he was not still a stranger, for all intents and purposes.

But she wanted to know more about him. She wanted answers to the riddle that was Mr. Calloway. "What was your history with him?"

"I believe he killed my best friend."

Her lips parted on a gasp. He'd made this accusation before, but it was no less shocking hearing it again.

"I grew up with Andrew Alston, who was Everley's cousin…and the rightful heir to the Everley title and the estate it was entailed to."

"Ah." It came out as a sigh as she pieced it together.

"Everley had never been kind to Alston. Their relationship was strained, at best. So when Everley invited him out to hunt…even then I was suspicious." Mr. Calloway looked down at his hands, lost in his memories. "Though I never suspected it would end in murder. It wasn't until I talked to other members of the hunting party and heard three different utterly inconsistent stories about how the 'accident' occurred that I really grew suspicious." He looked over to her. "Everley had the means, the motive… And I knew in my heart that he was responsible for taking my best friend from me, directly or indirectly."

"So you investigated further?" she prompted.

"I did, yes." His laugh was humorless and self-deprecating. "I made a hash of it. I bungled it all and made Everley look like the martyr." He scrubbed a hand over his face in a rare show of weariness that made her heart ache. "I never did find the evidence I was looking for, and in the process I made a handful of enemies." He met her gaze. "Including your father."

Her breathing stilled as she met his dark, serious gaze. "Because he was friends with Everley. They were..." She waved a hand. "Cohorts."

She didn't phrase it as a question and he did not answer.

He didn't have to.

She knew it to be true.

Her father was not a kind man, and she had little reason to believe he was honorable. It was becoming alarmingly apparent that he was not.

How much did her stepmother know of all this?

She shook off the question. What did it matter? Her stepmother was as powerless in her role as Delilah was in hers. Even if she'd suspected that Everley was a monster, she could not have done anything to prevent the engagement.

"To think," Delilah said, more to herself than to him. "If it wasn't for you, I would have married him without a second thought."

"You give *me* the credit?" he asked, a hint of amusement breaking the tension. "You would have realized eventually—"

"But not until it was too late."

He opened his mouth to argue the point, and she cut him off with a shake of his head. "I wouldn't have seen it sooner because I wouldn't have wanted to." Her voice hitched and she had to take a deep breath to continue. "I did not wish to see Everley for who he was, because it would have meant knowing that....that my father truly did not care."

He shifted closer, reaching for her to comfort her like he had yesterday, but she pulled back. "No. Wait, please. There is something I need to say."

He stilled, his brow furrowed and his dark gaze locked on hers as though there was nothing in the world more important than whatever it was she had to say.

"I owe you an apology." The words were stiff, her lips frozen. She and apologies had never been friends. She'd never quite gotten the hang of them, but at least she'd managed to get the words out.

He arched one brow in surprise but kept quiet as she'd asked. She smoothed her hands over her skirt in a nervous gesture. "When you offered to marry me last night—"

"Delilah—" he started

She spoke over him. "When you kindly offered to save my reputation by marrying me, I reacted horribly." She closed her eyes as shame swept over her again. "I was unforgivably rude, and I am sorry."

"You were under a great deal of stress."

She rolled her eyes at his attempts to justify her bad behavior. "Perhaps, but that was not why I seemed so...so..."

"Horrified?" he offered, that hint of amusement once again in his voice. He seemed to revert to amusement no matter what the circumstance, as though he were forever on the lookout for reasons to laugh—at himself, and at everyone around him.

Such a strange man.

A strange, gruff, kind, *wonderful* man.

A surge of affection for this brute had her looking away as heat stole over her.

Horrified, he'd said. That was the right word for her reaction, and yet it wasn't the truth. She hadn't been able to fathom it because...because...

She sighed. "I was raised to marry well."

He stayed silent beside her.

She peeked over at him with a smile she feared was bitter. "I was supposed to be a boy, you know."

He arched his brows. "Oh yes?"

She let out a huff of amusement at his tone. "I was a disappointment because not only did I kill my mother in childbirth, but I had the gall to be a girl as well."

He winced slightly, no doubt at the acidity in her tone. But it could not be helped. This man had been honest with her and had saved her at every turn. He deserved the unfettered truth.

"All I was ever meant to do was marry well. It was all I was good for in my father's eyes. I thought if I could at least do *that* than maybe..."

He'd love me. He'd think me worthy.

It was too depressing to say any of those aloud, but she assumed he understood without her spelling it out.

He squeezed her hand tightly and she let out a long exhale. "But I am beginning to see that perhaps his good opinion is not worth much. Not really. After all, why should *he* think well of *me* when *I* do not think well of *him*?"

He shifted, flipping her hand so he could hold it properly.

Well, *im*properly, as the case may be.

"Delilah, it is only natural to want to please your parents. To live up to their hopes and expectations."

She nodded. "I suppose you are right. But still..." She met his gaze. "I am sorry for the way I behaved when you offered to save me."

"Don't be," he said softly. "I completely understand." He paused. "I would have been horrified at the thought of marrying me, too."

A short laugh was shocked out of her at that and when she looked up and met those warm brown eyes that now twinkled with laughter, she felt a lightness steal over her and she laughed some more, him joining in this time.

For the first time in a long time, she felt...happy.

Which was ridiculous given the circumstances, but there it was. Sitting here, alone with this man, who seemed to understand her and perhaps even *like* her despite all her many flaws—or maybe because of them...

She felt at home. She felt welcome.

She felt...loved.

The thought had her chest constricting, her lungs emptying of air as the room seemed to shift around her.

It wasn't necessarily a *bad* feeling. No, this heady, dizzy sensation was almost...pleasant. She supposed it was how one felt when one imbibed too much sherry.

She felt positively intoxicated by the warmth that flooded her in his presence.

"I was wrong, though, when I said I could not marry you." She said it as lightly as she could manage once her heart resumed a normal beat. "It would be a privilege to be your wife."

His gaze intensified so quickly it made her heart race all over again and the air between them grew heavy and hot with anticipation.

Heat flooded her cheeks as her own words hit her. Heavens, how very forward of her. He must have thought... What if he believed she was saying...

Her voice came out too loud. "What I meant to say was that any woman would be honored—"

He cut off her words with a kiss. He'd moved so quickly she had not seen it coming, tugging her arm lightly so she tumbled toward him, her free hand catching herself against his chest as he wrapped his arm around her and pulled her closer so she was nestled against his side.

His kiss was heaven, all warmth and affection, passion and

tenderness, as his lips crushed hers with a force that made her heart thud painfully in response.

He pulled back slightly and rested his forehead against hers as they both breathed heavily. "Delilah, I—" He pulled back to look at her and wariness stole over his gaze.

"Yes?"

His chest rose and fell beneath her hands. "There is something I really ought to tell you..."

Nervous anticipation had her muscles contracting as if she could physically brace herself for whatever blow that was to come.

It *would* be a blow. His normally laid-back expression was replaced by a wariness that was unnerving. All amusement was gone from his eyes.

"Rupert, whatever it is, you can tell me," she said quietly.

He gave her a rueful little smile. "Delilah, I am..."

A bastard.

A merchant.

A pauper who inherited a lovely home.

"I am the second son of a marquess," he said on one long breath.

She blinked. "Pardon?"

Amusement once more crept into his gaze. "The Marquess of Markland," he said. "He is my father."

"*What?*" She pushed away from him. "But why...? How...?" Shock had her so flustered she could not even form a question.

His low laugh made her insides quiver and then she was back in his arms.

"Right," he said, satisfaction written all over his face. "Now that we've got that sorted..."

His kiss killed any questions she might have asked, and though she had questions that *would* be answered, for now... she was more than happy to let him kiss her instead.

13

"You mean, you did not *know* that he was a marquess's son?" Prudence asked. Her features were the picture of disbelief.

"You really had *no idea*?" Addie was laughing. Her little brother Reggie was laughing too though Delilah assumed he was not laughing at her.

She narrowed her eyes at the toddler. He'd better not be.

Her scowl made him giggle that much more.

Louisa was off with her family, or maybe her fiancé, since they rarely seemed to be parted these days. Good thing. Louisa would have been laughing so hard Delilah might have had to smack her.

She huffed. "You could have told me," she said to Addie.

Addie shrugged. "I didn't realize you did not know."

Prudence gave a little sigh of exasperation. "I suppose this means you like him now?"

Heat flooded Delilah's cheeks too quickly for her to hide it. She ducked her head all the same, feigning a great interest in the embroidery on her lap which had been doing nothing to hold her interest until just this moment.

Embarrassment mingled with shame. Embarrassment because—yes. Yes, she did like him.

Quite a bit, in fact.

Just the thought of him made her feel warm all over. And...*mushy*. Her insides had definitely taken to melting whenever she thought of him.

Most inconvenient as she'd been doing nothing but think about the man all day. She'd thought of him while taking breakfast in her room. She'd thought of him when he'd seen her to the school, all gruff charm as usual as though this was just another day.

As though he was not bound to slay her dragons this very evening.

He was all calm confidence as he bid her farewell as though he had not kissed her senseless the night before.

The other girls were strangely silent so she made a half-hearted attempt to jab a needle into her embroidery. She'd likely ruin the thing if she kept assaulting it like this, but what else was she to do with her restless hands as she waited for word that Rupert was all right?

She shifted uncomfortably, all too aware of Prudence's unwavering gaze.

Prudence knew her too well, at times. And her words still stung. *I suppose that means you like him now.*

Her friend wasn't trying to be cruel. She was just honest. She'd never hesitated on calling Delilah out on her moral flaws, and Delilah's selfish desire for status, power, and yes, wealth—well, it was legendary.

She'd embraced her reputation as the spoiled debutante, and now she was stuck with it.

Because it was still true.

Wasn't it?

"Delilah?" Addie's voice was gentle. "Are you all right?"

Delilah lifted her head with a smile. "Fine."

Addie still looked concerned. "They will be safe, you know."

Delilah nodded. Tolston was with Rupert, and they had a handful of men, as well. They'd left two men here to guard her and the others, although everyone agreed that with Everley at the docks and distracted by his business, the security was most likely an unnecessary precaution.

As Tolston had said before they'd left. Only a desperate man or a fool would attack Delilah here, tonight when she was surrounded by friends and in a good neighborhood.

And besides... If all went well, she would be back with Rupert in his home by the time the moon was high overhead.

A desperate tightness in her chest stole her breath away. She could not wait to be back home with Rupert safe at her side.

Prudence reached a hand out to cover hers. "Are you so very worried about him then?"

Delilah thought to make a quip, to toss aside her friend's concern. But in the end, she did not have the energy to feign nonchalance. "Yes."

The other two girls studied her in silence and Delilah let them. What was the point of pretending?

"You care about him." Prudence's comment might have been sweet if she did not so stunned.

Delilah scowled. "Of course I care about him. I just told you that he kissed me, did I not?"

Prudence's eyes went wide and she looked like an owl wearing those spectacles she only wore when embroidering or reading alone in her room. She might act all morally superior, but Prudence suffered her share of vanity.

"Yes, but I thought..." Prudence trailed off, her lips pursing in an expression befitting a peeved governess.

Addie leaned forward, stepping in as the peacemaker. "I think what Prudence meant was that she thought...that is, we believed..." She cleared her throat, casting a quiet look of desperation in Prudence's direction.

"We thought you allowed him to kiss you because you'd learned of his status," Prudence finished.

Delilah blinked as the words struck her chest. Of course her friends would think that. They would undoubtedly believe that she would only allow a man to kiss her so scandalously if she thought him to be proper husband material.

She had a sudden flash of Rupert's eyes—so warm with affection, his arms around her so secure and stable, his voice so low and amused even when she was saying all the wrong things. The type of things that typically drove people away.

He would be wonderful husband material, but not because of his honorary title.

Because of *him*.

She bit her lip as unexpected tears filled her eyes causing her friends to lean toward her with alarm.

"Dee?" Prudence said, shock replacing her judgmental scowl. "Are you all right?"

No. She was not all right. Because the man who'd kissed her, the gentleman who was at this very moment riding off into the night to fight her battle, the man who'd held her and comforted her and who seemed to understand her as no other ever had...

He *had* proposed the other night.

Sort of.

In a manner of speaking.

And she'd *rejected* him.

She blinked rapidly to try and push the unshed tears away but only managed to make them trickle over so she was swiping at her eyes in dismay.

"Delilah," Addie said slowly, gently. She shifted Reggie in her lap and used the same tone of voice she used when she was attempting to make her younger brother eat his peas.

"Did you kiss Mr. Calloway *before* you knew he was the son of a marquess?"

Delilah hesitated and then nodded.

Prudence let out a gasp more befitting a melodrama at the theater.

Delilah frowned at her friend. "Really, Pru, it is not *that* shocking."

Pru's wide eyes begged to differ.

Delilah huffed. "He kissed me before last night as well," she said. For some reason the truth was just pouring out of her tonight, and it was a relief. Focusing on Rupert and her feelings for him was better than wondering where he was now and what sort of danger he might meet upon his trip to the docks.

"When you believed him to be some sort of hired investigator?" Addie asked.

Delilah rolled her eyes. Was it really that difficult to understand? "Yes."

"Because you..." Prudence looked around the room as if searching for an answer. "Because you felt so indebted to him for saving your life?"

Delilah frowned at her friend. Prudence was going to make her say it aloud. "No, you ninny. Because I..." She swallowed. "Because I *like* him." She cleared her throat. "Quite a bit, actually."

So much so that the word 'like' felt completely wrong on her tongue. So mild and unfeeling as to be meaningless.

"I see," Prudence said.

It was clear that she did not.

But Addie did. The other girl was giving her a soft, sympathetic smile that spoke of understanding and empathy. "It is awfully overwhelming, is it not?"

Delilah shifted in her seat. "What is?"

"Falling in love."

Delilah's lungs stopped working. Her heart, on the other hand—her heart decided this was the moment to prove how hard it could work. It seemed like the organ might explode within her chest if it beat any harder.

Love.

Was this love?

She let out a long rush of air. Yes. That was precisely what this feeling was—the sensation that she'd forgotten herself entirely.

Or maybe that she'd found a new part of herself that she hadn't known existed.

All she knew was that it was terrifying, this sense of suddenly needing another human being. But it was also… rather lovely, in a way. Not the needing, and not the fearing for his safety, but the knowledge that she could care about someone so thoroughly and completely. So blindly.

More than that, that someone could look at her the way he did, as though she were perfect, even with all her plentiful flaws.

Whenever she acted badly, he seemed to find it amusing, like he could see right past her sharp tongue and her harsh words to the heart of her. Like he knew her so well that try as she might, she would never scare him away.

He looked at her like she had true value. Like she was priceless, even if she did not have a fortune to give or a plot of land to bestow with her dowry. He held her in his arms as though he could honestly care about her and…

Well, she hoped that meant he loved her.

He did, didn't he? He would not have kissed her, or offered to marry her, or taken such sweet care of her if he did not.

Right?

"Have you…" Prudence cleared her throat and shifted in her seat as though this talk of emotions made her ill at ease.

Likely true. Prudence was not one to talk about romance or love. Unlike Louisa who was smitten with romance novels, and Addie who'd been smitten with Tolston since she'd arrived at the school, Prudence was distinctly uncomfortable with all talk of love. She tilted her head to the side with feigned composure. "Have you discussed the future?"

Delilah winced as if her friend had struck her. "Not quite."

And right now that fact was killing her. Rupert had not mentioned marriage again after her disastrous response that first time.

And yet she'd let him kiss her.

And then she'd kissed him back.

Without a thought for her reputation or her future.

"Of course they haven't," Addie said with a sigh of exasperation. "Who could be concentrating on the future when Delilah's very life is in danger."

Delilah straightened at that and even Prudence looked a bit chastened at the reminder of what they were all doing here.

Waiting.

Delilah stood up with a start. "I cannot just sit here and embroider while Rupert is in danger." She shot Addie and accusing glare. "How can you be so complacent?"

Addie sighed. "I am not. I'm terrified, but I know that Tolston and the others are well armed and they have the advantage of surprise."

"Everley is not such a big man and he won't be traveling with an army if he wishes to remain inconspicuous." There were times when Prudence's teacherly voice grated on Delilah's nerves, but right now her didactic tone was reassuring.

She was right, of course. She and Addie likely had nothing to worry about.

It was just that Delilah would feel so much better when she saw Rupert again with her own two eyes.

And then she would demand that he marry her.

The thought struck her at once and was both ludicrous and...rather perfect, really. He ought to know better than to kiss a young lady without making promises. And she'd be sure that he did.

A nagging sensation in her gut told her she didn't wish for him to propose because he *had* to or because he was morally obliged...

But she did wish him to propose.

It did not matter how or why, merely that he *did*.

She scowled down at her toes. If he did not love her yet, she would just have to make him, that was all.

Her hands clenched into fists. She would make that man love her if it was the last thing she did.

"Oh, Delilah, there you are." Miss Grayson's normal calm elegance was nowhere to be seen as she rushed into the room, her skirts whipping around her legs with her quick pace. "There's a message for you from your home."

Delilah took the missive from her with a frown. A message from home? It had to be from her stepmother. A quick look at the penmanship confirmed it but the unusually messy scrawl had her pulse quickening with alarm.

"Your family's footman is waiting in the hallway," Miss Grayson murmured, her pretty features tight with concern as Addie, Prudence, and even Reggie came to their feet to watch her read it.

"It's my father," she said through lips that had grown numb. "He has taken another turn for the worse."

"Oh my heavens," Miss Grayson said.

She heard Prudence murmur a prayer under her breath.

For Delilah's part, a cold numbness swept over her as she

waited for tears that did not come. "She's asked me to hurry home, in case..."

She could not quite finish the sentence. *In case he dies tonight.* It was a strange emotion that clogged her throat and made speech temporarily impossible.

Sadness, yes. Grief, of course. But more than that it was regret.

Regret that she might lose her father this very night and she still only knew him as well as she might a distant uncle. Her memories of him accumulated to a handful of cold, loveless images, sounds, and interactions.

She looked down at the ground as she took a deep breath. But, even so, he was her father. And she would be there for him in his time of need.

"I must go," she said, already hurrying toward the door.

"Wait," Miss Grayson called out. "I cannot let you rush off alone. I will come with you."

"No, please," Delilah said. "You ought to stay here with the others. I will be safe in my own home."

Addie was frowning in concern as she worried her lower lip. "At least take one of Tolston's men as a guard. A precaution," she said quickly as Delilah went to protest.

Delilah hesitated. "But there are more of you here, and Everley believes that I am with you and—"

"Please." Miss Grayson reached for her hand. "As you said, there are more of us. If danger arises, we can battle Everley ourselves. But I don't like the thought of you alone on the road again with only your family's footman as your companion."

Delilah swallowed. Truth be told, she didn't like the thought of being on the road without Rupert. She only felt safe these days when he was at her side.

As if reading her thoughts, Addie gave her a small smile.

"Do it for our sake. I don't believe Mr. Calloway would ever forgive us if we let you leave here without a guard."

Delilah choked on a laugh that was inexplicably mixed with tears.

Strange how she couldn't quite summon tears for her father's imminent death, but the mere thought of Rupert's fear for her safety made her want to weep like a watering pot.

Perhaps because she knew for certain that whether he loved her or not, his fear for her safety was genuine. His feelings for her were sincere and they were deep...whether or not they included love.

Her heart swelled as she nodded. "Yes, all right. I will send word to let you know when I've arrived safely."

14

Most stakeouts were a tedious bore interspersed with the odd bit of action.

Luckily for Rupert, tonight was another story entirely.

Delilah's recounting of that diary entry was proven correct and Everley proved himself to be punctual...even when it came to crime.

"There he is," Tolston murmured. "Right on time."

Sure enough, they watched Everley exit an unmarked coach toward the end of the block before disappearing into a warehouse.

Tolston moved to open the door. "Let us get this over and done with so we can get back to our ladies."

Despite the circumstances, Rupert found himself battling a ridiculous grin. *Our ladies.*

He thought of Delilah.

My lady.

If she would have him. The thought made him hesitate for a second as he led Tolston and the other men to surround the warehouse in question.

She would say yes. She'd have to. Her reputation would be in tatters once word spread about her broken engagement. Even if the end of their betrothal was not her fault, there was no way she'd escape unscathed. She'd be tainted by scandal no matter how this night ended.

The thought had him growling low in his throat as he drew close enough inside the warehouse to spot Everley and the man he was to meet. A roughened chap—a sailor, most likely.

If he could, Rupert would murder Everley right here and now for what he'd done to Delilah. It was bad enough he'd nearly harmed her, but no matter how badly he paid for his crimes there was no avoiding the fact that Delilah would suffer because of her attachment to him, no matter how brief it might have been.

Marrying a marquess's son would help, but for the first time since he'd left high society he found himself regretting it. Oh, he loved his life of freedom and intrigue, but his renegade ways would do little to salvage Delilah's reputation among the *ton*.

He'd give anything to suddenly have the respect of the society he'd eschewed just so long as his bride received the same respect.

His bride. His lips twitched again with barely concealed giddiness and he was forced to chide himself. Now was definitely not the time to lose his head over a lady.

Even if she was *his* lady.

Even if she was his *love*.

He stilled behind a stack of crates as a fear that had been plaguing him struck him anew. What if she did not feel the same?

Oh, he knew that she was attracted to him—not even Delilah could fake that sort of passionate response to his kisses. And he suspected she liked him.

But did she love him?

Would she say yes when he proposed again? And if she did, would it be because she needed him or because she wanted him?

Did it matter?

Yes. Yes, it did.

Tolston's presence at his side brought him back to the moment. They were here for a job. One that would ensure Delilah's safety. Everything else could wait until she was safely in his arms, where she belonged.

Tolston gave a jerk of his head in a signal to move closer and Rupert nodded, gesturing for to the men who waited behind them. A separate group would be closing in on the exits on the other side of the building in case Everley tried to run.

"It's getting harder, my lord," the sailor was saying as they drew close enough to hear.

Everley—that cold cruel man—he looked utterly unconcerned as he looked over the shipment the sailor had led him to.

"Don't fret, Myers, it makes you look weak."

The other man stiffened. "Sir, I'm merely pointing out that my men and I nearly got caught coming all the way into port, and—"

"Yes, as you mentioned with the last shipment," Everley interrupted. "I told you then that I would handle it, did I not?"

The sailor shifted uneasily and Rupert shared a look with Tolston at Everley's cold impatience.

"I'll be inheriting a nice bit of land along the seaside soon enough, and our arrangement will resume under safer conditions."

Rupert stiffened. Delilah had told him the details of her dowry and it included some land along the coast.

But Everley had said *inherit*.

"My bride will gift me the land on the sea that I require, and her untimely death will give me everything else I need."

An icy fear gripped his heart as Rupert put the pieces together. The arranged marriage, his lack of attempt to woo her or even get to know her.

He'd never planned to keep her as his bride.

He just wanted to get the land that came with her dowry and then...what? Just kill her off? But why? Was he so very merciless? So undeniably evil?

Rupert's mind was racing ahead of him as his gut turned to a heavy weight and ice crept into his veins. Why would he go to so much trouble to marry her and then kill her?

It made no sense. Unless he had another bride in mind...

He'd stopped paying attention to the conversation but Everley's next words brought him back with a jolt.

"Do not worry about the details. The land will be mine as soon as I'm wed and now that I've been granted special license, I plan to get the deed done first thing in the morrow."

The sailor let out a cackle. "Then my best wishes to you, sir."

He planned to wed her tomorrow? Terror plagued him. If this man's plans included a wedding in the morning, he must have eyes on her. Did he know she was not at her home?

When he turned to face Tolston, the other man's face was set and determined as he jerked a head toward the door. *Go. Protect your woman*, his stern gaze seemed to say.

Rupert was just about to leap into action when the sailor spoke again. "You're marrying tomorrow and yet you're here with me. Ain't your bride-to-be waiting on you, my lord?"

Everley's smile was cold. "Do not fret about my bride. She is in good hands. As we speak, my partner is ensuring that she will be ready, willing, and able to marry me at first light."

My partner.

The words somehow felt more ominous than anything else Everley had said this night. Tolston had frozen as well and the other men were exchanging glances that held one question.

Who is Everley's partner?

Since when did he work with an accomplice? If he was telling the truth—and he had no reason not to be—then that meant they'd underestimated him. They hadn't properly planned. That meant he'd...

His heart plummeted into his stomach.

He'd left Delilah vulnerable.

He had to get to her. His mind was already working out the fastest way out of this warehouse without alerting Everley and his men to his presence. He could be out of here and back to the School of Charm before this partner had a chance to nab her.

"If your bride has any sense, she'll have run for the hills by now," the sailor said with another chuckle.

"If my bride had any sense, she'd have fled her own home years ago," Everley answered, his voice so mild. So uncaring. He was talking about Delilah like she was some stranger, someone of no worth or merit.

It made him want to shove a hand through the man's chest and rip out his cold, useless heart.

Rupert wanted to end her miserable father's existence while he was at it. He'd never thought well of the old man, not even as a child, and any respect he might have had for him died a quick death when the man promised his beautiful, surprisingly sweet, incredibly strong, and utterly vulnerable only daughter to this vile man.

But now, what Everley was suggesting...

Her father could not have known that Everley intended to kill her...could he?

"You're awfully sure of your partner," the sailor said.

"As well I should be," Everley said. "She is highly competent."

His head whipped to the side to meet Tolston's hard glare. *She*.

Everley had said...*she*.

And just like that it clicked. The only person it could be. The one woman who'd been there all along, negotiating Delilah's wedding and the dowry that would come with it.

The woman who'd sent Delilah off on her own in a carriage bound for her ruin.

Tolston edged toward the warehouse doors at the same time he did, and when they met outside, there was no debate about what next to do.

They had to protect their women.

Lord Tumberland met them as well. "What about Everley?" he asked.

Rupert shook his head. "If our men don't grab him tonight, we'll chase him down eventually."

Tolston added, "Between the shipment we saw tonight and what we heard, we have more than enough to prove that he's a criminal. But for right now..."

Rupert was already ahead of them, his blood pounding in his ears as panic and determination and a million emotions he never knew he could experience took over.

"You go to the school," he said to Tolston and Tumberland. "Make sure the ladies are safe."

"Where will you go?"

"Her family home," he said. "Just in case Everley is right and Delilah has been caught."

Tolston froze. "You think this partner he spoke of lives at her *home*?"

Rupert's jaw clenched in anger. "I know it."

Everything in him ached to head straight to the school.

She'd be at the school. She had to be. He was just being overly cautious by keeping an eye on her stepmother.

He'd make sure the stepmother was not a threat, and then he'd go to her. He'd seek her out at the school, and when he found her there safe and sound...

Well, then he wouldn't let her out of his arms until she promised to marry him.

15

Delilah stared at the man lying unconscious on the ground before her, her mouth bone dry with horror. "Is he..." She tried to swallow. "Is he *dead*?"

"Hmm?" Her stepmother looked up from the letter she was reading as that blasted clock ticked away the hour. Her gaze fell on Delilah's guard who'd been unceremoniously attacked and felled the moment they'd entered the house.

The baroness sniffed. "Really, Delilah. I never took you to be so morbid. Of course he is not dead."

Delilah continued to stare at the man's back, hoping to see some movement that would indicate breathing. She was not convinced her stepmother was correct.

"I never thought you to be one for dramatics either." Her stepmother huffed as she set the letter down. "But first sneaking around your fiancé's private study and then rushing off with your knight in shining armor like some sort of slattern." She made a tsking noise as Delilah's jaw fell.

Her mind was still struggling to catch up but she could not quite reconcile this new turn of events. It did not help that, aside from her guard's attack, her visit to her family home felt absurdly...normal. The drawing room was still filled with that cloying scent, the servants still cowered in silence and ignored what was going on around them.

That blasted clock still ticked too loudly in the otherwise too-quiet room.

And yet...

She stared down at the man who'd been told to keep her safe.

He still had not moved.

"My father," she started slowly, feeling like an absolute imbecile for having to ask. "His health..."

"Is the same as ever." Her stepmother's normally cool voice was laced with irritation. "Stubborn man. The old goat refuses to die." Her mother's sudden smile caught her off guard and she blinked. "But that's all right. It's for the best that he hung on this long. Just long enough for you to marry the man of my choosing."

Delilah blinked again. "*Your* choosing?"

Her stepmother let out a short humorless laugh. "Delilah, dear. Your father has barely been alive, let alone awake, for two years now. You did not think that he had a hand in your betrothal, now did you?"

Delilah's mouth opened but no sound came out.

"I've been handling all the decisions around here for a long time now." Her eyes were hard when they landed on Delilah. "I've been running this household, raising his spoiled brat of a daughter, ensuring sure his properties are making money as his mind failed him. I've been doing it all...and for what?" She leaned forward. "Do you have any idea what your father left me in his will?"

Delilah swallowed and shook her head.

"Nothing," her stepmother hissed. "A paltry allowance, barely fit for a pauper. Whatever was not entailed all goes to you and your precious dowry." She sneered those last words, years of disdain finally breaking through that icy façade. "The land by the sea, the money...it's all wrapped up in your dowry, you ungrateful little cur."

Fear was stealing over her, finally...belatedly. She should have been terrified the moment she'd entered and realized that there was no doctor here, and then she should have screamed in horror when her stepmother's footman and carriage driver took her guard down from behind.

She ought to have been fearful from the start, but she hadn't because...this was home. And her stepmother had been as placid and cool as ever. They'd sat together in silence like they'd done a hundred times before as they waited for the carriage to be brought 'round to take them to a soiree or a ball.

But now...

Now her stepmother's words were beginning to register and understanding dawned. Her stepmother had formed an alliance with Everley. She'd been behind this from the start.

Running off with your knight in shining armor. She knew about the carriage accident and, what was more...she knew about Rupert.

That was what finally had terror setting in. Too late, perhaps, but at least she could say the fear was on behalf of another.

For an ungrateful, spoiled brat she supposed that was something to brag about. She probably ought to be worried about her own safety, but all she could think about was Rupert.

Was he safe? Had he found Everley?

Would he finally get his revenge?

Her gaze settled once more on the stranger who lay at her feet, seemingly forgotten by her stepmother.

Just so long as Rupert was safe. That was what mattered.

As for her...

She took a deep breath and lifted her head. Years of practice had her sliding into the role she'd adopted a lifetime ago. Leaning back in her seat, she squared her shoulders and feigned a bored apathy. "What do you plan to do with me now?"

"You'll marry Everley, of course," her stepmother said. "As planned."

She too seemed to have caught herself and settled once more back into the role *she'd* perfected. Cool, calm, unperturbed, and unfeeling.

"How will that benefit you?" Delilah asked. "If I become Everley's wife and he obtains the dowry..." Her voice trailed off as ice stole through her veins.

Delilah knew. Of course she figured it out. She was spoiled, perhaps, but not stupid.

Her stepmother gave her a small smile and Delilah caught a flash of triumphant cruelty in those beautiful blue eyes. "You will not be his wife for long."

"He will murder me," Delilah whispered. Her stepmother did not confirm the matter, but she did not need to. "He will end me and you will take my place."

"Once your father finally dies, yes," she said. Her eyes were starting to glow with pleasure. "And then all that ought have been mine, will be."

It was clear that her stepmother was glad to be telling her this. Despite her calm, Delilah sensed a shift in her stepmother. A new energy.

Elation, perhaps. Triumph, definitely.

She'd won, and she knew it.

Meanwhile, Delilah hadn't even known they'd been at war.

How odd.

The clock ticked the seconds, and Delilah shivered despite herself at the ominous sound. It was a monotonous countdown to the final moments of her life. And then it clicked. Her slow, shock-addled brain made the connection at last. "You were behind the carriage incident."

Her stepmother smiled as though Delilah were a dull student who'd finally gotten the right answer. "Yes, that was me. Well, that was me and Everley." Her smile turned affectionate. "He and I make for a wonderful partnership. At long last I've found someone who respects my intellect and understands my worth."

Delilah nearly choked on bile at the thought of her stepmother and Everley plotting her murder together as some sort of romantic interlude.

Her stepmother's smile faded. "But again with the melodrama. You would not have been killed." Her lips curved in a momentary sneer. "I would not have cried if you *were*, but it was not part of the plan."

Delilah forced herself to refrain from reacting.

"No," her stepmother said with a weary sigh. "We could not have you die before Everley got your dowry, otherwise all that money and the land Everley needs would end up being passed along to your father's heir." She leaned forward. "Even if you'd died, I would still not get what I deserved." She narrowed her eyes. "Your father never knew what he had in me. He married me and then treated me like I was the hired help. I was *your* nursemaid and then *his*." She trailed off with a sound of disgust.

"If you did not intend to kill me..." Delilah started.

"Well, we could not have you prodding about and stirring up trouble, now could we?" The baroness made it sound so normal. So reasonable. Like they were discussing what dessert to serve at their next soiree. "They would not have killed you, dear." Her lips curved up slowly. "Though they might have ruined you."

Delilah fought a shiver at the sheer delight in her stepmother's eyes.

She'd never fooled herself into thinking her stepmother loved her. She'd never even believed she liked her.

But she'd had no idea the baroness hated her.

"I'll admit, it would have been a treat to watch the spoiled, perfect daughter be ruined in society..." She sighed regretfully before leaning forward eagerly. "But perhaps you were?" Her eyes lit with an eager glow. "We never did find out who saved you that day, only that he looked like a ruffian." She clasped her hands together gleefully. "Your precious Miss Grayson might have lied on your behalf but my spies told me you never returned to the school that night. So tell me, *princess*..." She sneered the nickname that her father had given her as a child. "Did my dreams come true? Did the precious princess finally suffer?"

Finally? *Finally?* She swallowed down a wave of rage that felt blessedly good after being so frozen in fear. Did this woman truly think she'd never suffered?

She'd spent a lifetime in a household that held no love, and yet her stepmother believed that she'd gone through life without hardship?

She might have been spoiled with material goods, but she'd have given all of that up for a kind word from her stepmother. For a hint of attention or affection from her father.

She shoved the bitter thoughts aside and focused on what mattered.

Rupert.

She might have been caught by her stepmother, and she held little hope of escaping with her stepmother's men on the prowl. But Rupert was out there, and he would stop Everley, and more than that...

Her stepmother did not know who he was.

He was not in imminent danger so long as he stayed at the docks and dealt with Everley.

Her spine stiffened as she faced down her stepmother as she had a million times before. Delilah could handle the baroness, just so long as Rupert was safe.

Her stepmother was waiting for an answer. "I hate to disappoint you, but the man who rescued me proved to be a gentleman at heart. Far more of a gentleman than the man you'll be marrying upon my demise."

She said it sweetly, serenely. For once her sharp tongue and haughty manners served her well.

Delilah caught a flare of fury before her stepmother could cover it.

Had she always been this angry behind that cool façade?

Had she always been so...*insane?*

She suspected yes. Although, perhaps this was the result of years' worth of mistreatment at the hands of her father. She, too, had been ignored and undervalued.

Even so, Delilah couldn't quite summon up any pity, what with her life being threatened and all.

"You have no idea what sort of man Everley is," her stepmother said once she'd regained her composure. "He is a true nobleman—he takes what he wants, and he uses his power to help those he loves."

The way her eyes shone made it clear that she believed he loved her.

Delilah leaned forward. "Tell me, my lady, has it ever occurred to you that your precious Lord Everley might just be using you to get to me?"

Her stepmother blinked and then that cold façade slipped so fast Delilah stiffened in shock. She didn't move away quickly enough though, and her stepmother's instant fury came out with a swift slap to her cheek that left her head reeling. The side of her face throbbed but even so, a stab of satisfaction had her grinning.

"How do you know he will keep his promise and marry you?" she continued as if she hadn't been interrupted with a slap. This time she moved back, out of her stepmother's reach. "How do you know he will not leave you even more desperate and alone than you already are?"

Her stepmother's face turned a motley red as she lunged out of her settee—the composed baroness nowhere to be seen as he reared toward her. "You ungrateful little—"

Her words were cut off with a screech and Delilah lowered the hands she'd held up in defense as she watched her stepmother be unceremoniously picked up of her feet, her arms and legs swinging wildly as she shrieked.

"That's enough of that," Rupert said mildly.

Delilah's jaw went slack and her eyes grew wide at the sight of Rupert towering over her, her stepmother dangling from beneath one arm like she weighed nothing at all.

His furrowed brow and darkened eyes were filled with a devastating fury. "Are you all right?"

She nodded quickly. "Y-yes."

His gaze fell to her cheek and his eyes narrowed. He seemed oblivious to the shrieking going on just beneath his arm as her stepmother cried for help.

"I wouldn't bother," Rupert responded. "Your men have been dealt with."

Delilah let out a sigh of relief and pointed to her guard. "Your man, is he…?"

With one foot, Rupert rolled him over and the man groaned. "He will live."

"And you?" she asked, her voice high and uncertain. "What happened with Everley? Why are you here? How did you know?" The questions came tumbling out.

He gave her a small smile filled with affection. "I will tell you all just as soon as you are home and safe."

She nodded. *Home.* Her mind called up an image of his parlor, of his arms wrapped around her. Her breath caught in her throat. That was her home...

She glanced up at the big brute who was carting her still-shrieking stepmother out of the room.

Her home was with *him.*

She just hoped that he knew it.

16

Rupert was certain this dreadful night would never end.

He watched Delilah closely as he, Tolston, and his men rehashed the events of the evening and put a plan of action in place to ensure the baroness was punished for her part and Everley was caught.

The first light of dawn was starting to stream through the School of Charm's windows when he walked over to where Delilah sat, surrounded by her friends.

She looked tired, but otherwise unharmed.

His hands clenched at his sides as rage threatened to consume him again. The entire ride to her home, he'd panicked about what he might find. His mind had raced incessantly, imagining every hideous scenario, every heartbreaking ending to a love story they had not yet written.

When Rupert stopped before her, he saw her friends exchange a meaningful look before making their excuses. Once alone, she looked up at him with a wan smile before patting the seat beside her.

He sat and his heart warmed when she leaned slightly so she was resting against him.

He tucked his head to hide a grin. She was comfortable with him, of that there was no doubt. She felt safe with him, and that fact he adored.

But did she know that she was loved by him?

"How are you holding up?" he asked. He ached to slip an arm around her shoulders and pull her closer still but despite the bizarre circumstances, they were still surrounded by people and there was only so much scandal she could weather in one night.

She sighed wearily. "Do you mean, how am I holding up now that my fiancé and stepmother failed to marry me off for my fortune and then murder me?"

He winced at hearing her say it aloud like that. "Yes, that's what I meant."

"I suppose I am doing as well as one could hope." She tilted her head back to smile up at him. "Have I thanked you yet for rescuing me from my wicked stepmother the way you did?"

He laughed. "One or two times."

In truth, she'd thanked him no less than twenty times on the carriage ride back to the school. The moment her stepmother and her men were trussed up to await their punishment and they were alone, she'd thrown her arms around his neck and the thanking had begun.

He'd enjoyed it, no doubt, but it wasn't her gratitude he wanted.

"I wonder if my father was aware…" she said softly.

He reached for her hand. "I went up to his room while questioning his servants." He shook his head. "I do not think your father was aware of anything going on around him. And who knows how long he's been like that."

She pressed her lips together. "*I* should have known."

"How could you have?"

"I should have suspected. The fact that my father never left his rooms, that she never allowed me to see him, that she handled every correspondence and managed the household..." She sighed. "I thought he just did not wish to see me."

He stayed silent as she got lost in her thoughts. "I always knew the baroness was unhappy. I understood she did not like me. I just didn't realize she hated me quite so much."

This time Rupert did give in to the urge to comfort her. Ignoring the others in the room he wrapped an arm around her shoulders and held her close. "You deserved better. As a child and as a young lady, you deserved so much more."

Her smile trembled a bit. "Thank you, but...I don't know that that's true." He watched her with concern as tears welled up in her eyes. "How do you know what you're worth, what you are owed, what your value is when all you've ever been worth was the sum of your dowry and the appearances that will surely fade?"

He opened his mouth to reply but stopped when she shut her eyes tightly and shook her head. "Do not answer that. And please, don't listen to me. I'm being maudlin." When she opened her eyes again, they were wet with tears and a tremulous, rueful smile was back in place. "I suppose learning about one's planned murder will do that."

He gave a choked laugh at her gallows' humor. "I suppose so."

She shifted so she was facing him head-on. "What of Everley?"

"He has been caught." That was one of the reasons they'd been up all night, waiting and coordinating.

Her sigh of relief had her shoulders slumping forward and he tugged her close. She stiffened for only a moment before relaxing against his side, her head on his shoulder.

"Rest, my love," he murmured into her hair. "You are safe now."

"We should not...the others..." She started to stir and he kissed the top of her head.

"The others are studiously looking the other way," he informed her truthfully. Even Miss Grayson was making a show of calling for the servants and asking what refreshments everyone needed. "If ever there is a time propriety could be thwarted, this is it."

He felt her laugh more than heard it. "Says the man who's made a life out of thwarting propriety." Her tone was filled with amusement, and no heat, but the truth of it still stung.

He had given up propriety along with everything else when he eschewed the honorary title and his place within society.

At the time he'd given no thought to marriage, or that one day he might meet a lady who cared about such things. Who might deserve more than a hired investigator as a husband and a life on society's sidelines.

Regret hit him in the gut. Could she be happy with a man such as him?

Would he want her to sacrifice her dreams for power in society and balls and gowns and whatever else it was young ladies of the *ton* wished for?

He'd said it before and his words rung in his ears now. *She deserves more.*

His thoughts were cut short by the feel of her hand tentatively touching his chest. "I cannot believe that you left without Everley." She shook her head as if in disbelief, pulling back to look at his face. "You have spent so many years trying to make that man pay, and you had your chance—"

"He will still pay," Rupert cut in shortly, his voice choked with emotion that she worried about something like that.

That she could think for one second that his quest for revenge meant more to him than she did.

He reached a hand out to gently cup her chin. "Everley *will* pay, and dearly, for all that he did to you, what he planned to do, what he's done to so many others...he will pay for what he did to Alston."

"You could have had him," she said. "He was right there, along with the evidence. You could have had him and you walked away." She licked her lips, her voice tremulous. "You walked away for me. To save me."

"Of course I did." His response was quick, short, and more gruff with unchecked emotion than he'd anticipated.

Her eyes grew wide and her lips parted in surprise.

"Never doubt for one instant that you mean more than all of that. You wonder at your value, but I need you to know..." He stroked her cheek as his chest tight with emotions. "To me, you are more precious than anything else. You mean more than any revenge or any professional goals. You are..." His voice dipped as her eyes darkened. "Delilah, to me, you are *everything*."

Her eyes were so wide and so...tear filled.

Terror shot through him that rivaled anything he'd ever felt while working an investigation. Was it possible she did not feel the same?

Or perhaps things were different now that she was no longer dependent on him for safety, now that the threat she faced was gone...

Perhaps she was realizing that she was no longer promised to Everley, that she might be able to step into the light where she belonged.

She could have her pick of men once the scandal subsided. Gentlemen of the *ton* who would give her the life she'd always wanted.

"Rupert, I—I—"

"Your man has arrived!" Tolston shouted this news from across the room and it startled Delilah so badly that she shot out of his arms, scrambling backwards to put some distance between them as the others turned to stare.

His man. It took a moment for the words to register. His man who'd captured Everley and sent word that he'd be bringing him here.

"Go," she said, prodding him with a little shove to his arm. "Go see if you got your man and the justice you've been seeking."

He lingered, torn between staying with Delilah, making sure she was all right, and going off to make sure the man who would harm her was under his control along with his wretched partner.

"Delilah will be in good hands, Mr. Calloway," Miss Grayson said, coming to stand beside Delilah and placing a hand on her shoulder.

His heart begged him to stay, but his mind told him it was time to leave. To walk away.

He would be back to win her heart, but not until she was rested and healed and...

Well, she might never be ready to hear what he had to say. But he could at the very least resist the urge to push her on the matter until she'd had the chance to sleep.

"Take care of yourself, Delilah," he murmured as he leaned down to kiss her hand.

Take care of my precious heart.

17

Take care of yourself.

Delilah jabbed her needle into the fabric with more force than was absolutely necessary. Take care of herself.

For how long?

She stirred restlessly, unreasonably irritated by the calm contentedness of the friends who surrounded her.

The Beaumonts were hosting a ball tonight and by all rights, everyone here should be getting ready to attend. But Louisa, Addie, Prudence, and Miss Grayson had all declined without a question just to be here with her.

Delilah might have been able to go, but with all the chaos going on this week surrounding her stepmother and Lord Everley...there was no saying just how badly her reputation would be affected.

The gossips would be hard at work trying to sort out what exactly had happened that sent the baroness out of the country a ruined disgrace or why Lord Everley was being hauled off to prison.

The truth would undoubtedly come out in the newspapers soon enough, and Tolston had assured her once again earlier today that her name would be kept out of it as much as possible.

That was a good thing, she supposed. Perhaps she would get through to the other side with just a bit of scandal clinging to her name and not outright ruination.

She jabbed her needle once more. Yes, she should be very grateful, all things considered.

She should be pleased beyond reason that the entire ordeal was over and done with. Lord Tumberland had taken it upon himself to ensure that her father was being properly cared for and that his estate was being managed by reputable, trustworthy solicitors. Tolston had assured her that he still had men keeping an eye on the school on the off chance that Everley had accomplices who might seek revenge.

She'd been lucky indeed that, aside from her stepmother, it seemed no one knew that she had spent several evenings unchaperoned in a bachelor's home, so all in all...

She'd managed to escape this ordeal with nothing more than a sore cheek from her stepmother's attack.

She was very lucky.

All of these reasons to be grateful and glad. She stabbed the fabric one more time before throwing it to the side with an unladylike growl. "Where *is* he?"

Every head lifted at once and all eyes were on her, but no one pretended to misunderstand, thank goodness. She would have whipped the hide of anyone who dared to utter '*who?*'

"He will come to visit soon, I am sure of it," Louisa said. Her normally cheerful smile had been replaced by a worried expression that seemed to belie her words.

"Of course he will," Addie said.

Miss Grayson wore a kind smile but said nothing.

Delilah looked to Prudence who wore a familiar pursed-lipped look of disapproval which was aimed at Louisa and

Addie. "He has not come yet, I do not see why you'd expect him to come at all." She turned her attention back to the embroidery in her hands. "He has no business with Delilah now that the sordid affair has concluded. If he has not come yet..." She shot Delilah a sidelong look and the disapproval was gone. A flicker of sympathy and understanding flickered in her eyes. "Perhaps it is best to keep your expectations in check."

"Pru!" Louisa chided. "Why must you be so discouraging?"

Prudence shrugged. "I am merely pragmatic."

Delilah sighed. It was true. She was. Most of the time, Delilah appreciated that quality in Prudence. Unlike dreamy Louisa or optimistic Addie and kindhearted Miss Grayson, Prudence's black-and-white view of the world was often refreshing.

But not today.

Delilah scowled at her friend. "Could you at least try to find something positive to say?"

Prudence met her gaze evenly as she seemed to ponder the question. "You are alive and well thanks to Mr. Calloway. Is that not positive enough for you?"

Delilah blinked, the meaning hitting home. *Spoiled brat. Ungrateful cur.*

She swallowed and looked down at her embroidery, barely seeing the ivy pattern she'd been tediously working on as unexpected tears swam in her eyes.

Perhaps she was spoiled, and selfish, and ungrateful, and every other bad thing she'd ever been accused of being.

But she meant to change all that. She *wanted* to change, and for a little while there with Rupert, she'd felt like she was changing. The way he saw past all that, the way he challenged her to move beyond the behavior she'd learned as a child...

Yes, she had changed. And she would continue to change...with or without him.

She blinked and a traitorous tear fell. She swiped at it as her heart ached painfully in her chest.

She'd just prefer to change *with* him, that was all.

The settee sank beside her and Pru's hand covered her own. "I am sorry, Dee," she said softly. "I spoke without thinking. Of course he will come for you."

She did not truly believe it and hearing Prudence be disingenuous out of sympathy was almost more than she could bear.

"I really like him, Pru." It came out as a whisper and Prudence clutched her hand tighter.

"I know."

"I maybe even…" She swallowed convulsively. "Love him."

"Oh, Delilah," Prudence sighed.

The sympathy in Pru's voice made her want to weep. Her throat grew so tight she couldn't swallow and her chest…her chest felt like it might explode from emotion.

But she would not cry.

Quite frankly, she was tired of crying.

All week she'd found herself bursting into tears at the most inconvenient moments, and every time one of her friends or Miss Grayson had rushed to comfort her. But she was so tired of it. It was as though a lifetime of hurts and snubs and being ignored was all coming out this week and she was so tired of it.

She was exhausted from it, truth be told.

Louisa had told her it was good. Healthy, even. That she'd been in dire need of an emotional purge—that was Louisa's term for it—and that she'd feel lighter and happier for it in the end.

Delilah didn't feel either of those things.

She might have been letting go of her old grievances but with each passing hour that Rupert ignored her existence, her heart was breaking.

Maybe he'd been swept up in the excitement of it all. Passions had been running high. It was only natural that he'd get carried away. Maybe even say things that he did not mean.

Her heart pounded furiously at the thought of it.

Delilah, to me, you are everything.

She inhaled swiftly as her heart clenched painfully at the memory.

No. She refused to believe that he'd said all that out of some temporary sense of elation. She pulled her hand out from beneath Pru's and straightened her shoulders.

If he *had* then...

Well, who did he think he was?

Irritation spread through her at the thought and the urge to cry lessened.

Yes, anger was good. Anger made her feel less hopeless and more in control.

Anger good. Heartbreak bad. That was the simple thought that had her frowning at her friend. "What kind of gentleman goes spouting off romantic things like that and then flees for days on end?"

Pru's brows shot up in surprise and the others in the room turned their attention her way.

She made a show of arranging her skirts, her head held high and proud. "He had no right to say those things he said if he did not intend to court me."

Her friends were all staring at her wide-eyed.

"He should never have opened his mouth if he did not mean to marry me," she continued, anger coursing through her and making her feel like herself for the first time in days. She was no watering pot, and she never had been.

Righteous anger had her coming to stand, her arms crossed in indignation. "What kind of man makes a woman fall in love with him if he doesn't plan to marry her?" she demanded.

A servant opened the door to the drawing room but she ignored them. She was on a roll. "He had no *right* to make me fall in love with him. It was indecent and despicable and—"

"Beyond my control, I'm afraid." Rupert's voice in the doorway had her whipping her head to see him standing there, just behind the elderly housekeeper, whose eyes were wide with shock.

Delilah's heart leapt in her chest at the sight of him standing there—the same gentleman she remembered, but also...different.

His hair was shorn neatly and his clothes were fine and well-cut. His seemingly permanent stubble was shaved and he was...

Devastatingly handsome.

No. She straightened. He was *handsome*, but still the same brute who'd left her here without a word for nearly a week.

His grin was infuriating and smug.

He'd heard.

She narrowed her eyes in anger. Good. She was glad he'd heard. Her heart might have been racing away with excitement but she clung to her anger. Because if she was wrong...

If he wasn't here for the reason she hoped...

She huffed loudly and stomped her foot. "You had no right," she snapped.

His smile never wavered and she clenched her hands into fists as her palms tingled with the urge to rush over and smack him.

"Ladies," he said politely, his gaze never leaving Delilah's. "Would it be alright with you if I have a moment alone with Miss Clemmons?"

Miss Grayson was the first one out of her seat, grinning broadly as she rushed the others out of the room. "I'll just be..." she started as she pulled the door halfway shut behind them. She seemed to realize that neither of them were listening because she added softly. "Holler if you need me, dear," before slipping out of the room.

The door was open and she knew without a doubt that her friends hovered nearby, but they were for all intents and purposes...alone.

Her heart was beating so quickly she had to fight the urge to clap a hand to her breast to hold it in place.

"What are you doing here?" she snapped. It came out far angrier and much less desperate than it had sounded in her head. That was a relief.

His smile faded a bit and he moved toward her. Slowly. Cautiously.

Smart man.

When he came close enough that he could reach out and touch her, he stopped. "I am sorry I stayed away so long."

She glared at him. Did he really think that would suffice? She clamped her lips shut, telling herself she would not say another word until he gave her some sort of explanation.

He looked down at his boots—well-polished and seemingly new. "I, uh...I was afraid...."

"You were afraid?" she echoed, her voice rising alarmingly. She took a deep breath and tried again. "You, the man who has devoted his life to chasing after criminals and who singlehandedly took down Lord Everley—"

"I would not say singlehanded—"

"You were afraid?" she continued as if he hadn't interrupted, her voice filled with disbelief. "Of what? *Me?*" Something inside her slipped a bit. Some of that righteous anger faltered with the realization that perhaps he *had* been afraid of her.

Her own gaze dropped now so she was the one studying the toes of her slippers. "I know I am not exactly..." She flailed her hands as she sought the right word. "Approachable." She shifted uncomfortably. "I may not be as delicate or…demure as most ladies of your acquaintance, but I don't see—"

His fingers beneath her chin, tilting her face up, made her words freeze in her throat.

His grin was all rueful amusement. "Delilah, I am not afraid of *you*. If you'd let me finish, I was going to explain that I wanted to give you time and space so you could think and reconcile yourself to everything that had happened."

She blinked up at him dazedly, her mind struggling to sift through his words, searching for hidden meanings or something that might hurt her.

It was difficult to use reason at all when he touched her like this. All her mind wanted to do was focus on the feel of his rough, calloused fingertips on the sensitive skin of her cheek as he held her face in his hands now, cupping her jaw like she was some fragile, cherished treasure.

"I was afraid…" He gave a little sigh of impatience as he shook his head. "I did not mean to make you worry or to hurt you in any way. I merely wanted to give you room so you could sort out your feelings for me without the heightened emotions that can come with the sort of ordeal you just underwent."

Much as it pained her, she took a step back until his hands dropped. She needed a little distance to make sense of that. Once she did, his reasoning clicked with a startling clarity. "You thought I would have said yes to you because I was grateful."

His smile was small and a little too sad for her liking. "Something like that." He moved closer but kept his hands to himself. "I did not want you to make a hasty decision you might regret."

She blinked up at him, shaking her head in confusion as a million emotions flooded through her at once.

He wanted her. He was only looking out for her. He was afraid she'd reject him.

"Why would I regret choosing to be with you?" she asked. "I...I care about you."

He groaned as he moved toward her, this time taking her in his arms and pulling her close. "Do you, really, my love?" He pressed his lips to her temple. "Were you in earnest when I walked into this room? Did you really fall in love?"

Her lips quivered with a smile as ridiculous tears swam in her eyes. And yet, it was a smack she delivered to his chest as she pulled back to meet his gaze. "Of course, I love you. Do you think I let just any man kiss me?"

His grin toward roguish as he held her tighter still. "I hope I am the only man who ever has the privilege of kissing you." He leaned down and pressed his lips to hers, his soft groan making her want to weep because it echoed the same desperation she'd been feeling all week.

And here, now... She finally had him where she wanted him.

Kissing her, holding her—and he'd better not even *think* of ever letting go.

When at last he pulled back to meet her gaze, they were both breathless and holding one another tight.

"That wasn't the only reason I stayed away," he said quietly. He stroked a hand over her hair, likely mussing it but she found she did not care. His gaze was unnervingly serious, his eyes deliciously dark with emotion.

She steeled herself for whatever he might say, still wary of the happiness that threatened to drown her if she gave into it. "What is it?" she asked.

He dropped down to one knee as he clutched her hands in his.

"Rupert, what are you—"

"I want you by my side, Delilah. Now. Always. Forever."

Her heart exploded with joy. Tears overflowed and she was unable to keep the tide at bay any longer. That happiness swept over her so fast, so fierce, it left her trembling. "I want the same," she said. Tugging him to stand, she kissed him with all of the emotion she was feeling.

The kiss turned desperate as her lips clung to his. Her tears mixed with the taste of him and he pulled back abruptly.

"I love you, Delilah. I wish to make you my wife. However..."

She pulled back as well with a sudden frown. "What 'however'? Why a 'however'?"

He gave a short laugh as he wrapped his arms tightly about her waist. "Let me finish. I merely realized that you deserve better."

"Better than you?" Her frown intensified. "Never. No such thing exists. Not for me."

He tipped his head back with another laugh before he met her gaze with eyes filled with more affection than she'd ever imagined seeing in her entire life. "I do love you, you know that, yes?" he said. "Your strength is incredible and your belief in me is heartening. But what I'm trying to say is— falling in love with you, it has changed me."

Her eyes widened, because his words so perfectly echoed what she'd been feeling earlier. "Maybe that's what love does," she says. "It changes you."

"It made me want to be the sort of man you deserve," he continued.

Her eyes flickered over the clean-shaven jaw, the handsome new clothes and the perfectly groomed hair. "I don't care about all that," she said softly. "Not really."

"Maybe not, but I want to make you proud. I've talked to my father about reclaiming the honorary title, and about rejoining society with you at my side—"

"Rupert!" Her voice was high with irritation and amusement and giddy happiness. "You do not need to do all of this. Not for me. I may have been raised to believe that a 'good' match was all that mattered, but I know better now. I want a love match. I want a real match. I want...you." Her voice fell to a whisper as emotion choked her and the full force of the love in his eyes struck her. "That is all that matters."

He studied her for a moment with eyes so warm with affection it made her want to weep. "Perhaps you are right. But meeting you, falling in love with you, I suppose I realized that my dreams for the future have changed as well. Once upon a time, all I wanted wasF justice and revenge. I thought family and love would never mean as much to me as the call to right the wrongs of the ne'er-do-wells who walk among the elite."

She arched her brows. "And now?"

He sighed. "Now... Now I want to let go of the anger that drove me to this line of work. I will still take on the occasional investigation but I no longer relish the idea of risking the lives of those close to me, or even my *own* life...not when I have so much to live for."

"So..." She reached up and threaded her fingers through the edges of his new haircut. "You have turned a new leaf then."

He grinned. "It would seem so." Arching his brows, he lowered his voice. "All that being said, I cannot promise that I will avoid adventure entirely—"

"I should hope not!" she interjected pertly.

He laughed and tugged her closer, so she was enveloped in his arms. "But something tells me that a marriage to you...?" He dropped a sweet kiss to her lips. "That will be the greatest adventure of all."

ABOUT THE AUTHOR

MAGGIE DALLEN IS the author of more than a hundred romantic comedies in a range of genres including young adult, historical, and contemporary. An unapologetic addict of all things romance, she loves to connect with fellow avid readers. Come say hello on Facebook or Instagram!